Tale

Enid Blyton

Tales From The Bible

Illustrated by Eileen Soper

ARMADA

First published in the UK in 1944 by
Methuen & Co. Ltd
Republished by Dragon in 1970
This Armada edition 1988

Armada is an imprint of the Children's Division,
part of the Collins Publishing Group,
8 Grafton Street, London W1X 3LA

Copyright reserved 1944 by Enid Blyton

Printed and bound in Great Britain by
William Collins Sons & Co. Ltd, Glasgow

Preface

The Bible is full of fine, dramatic stories which hold a great appeal for children. The finest and most moving of all is, of course, the story of the life of Christ. This I have retold for children in 'The Children's Life of Christ.' Now I have taken the Old Testament and made my choice of stories there.

This book contains only tales from the Old Testament, and I have chosen all those which hold the greatest appeal for children. The Bible is literature, as well as history and a basis for religious beliefs, and, whether parents wish their children to be brought up religiously or not, probably most of them would want them to known the Old Testament stories – but not directly from the Bible itself.

I say this because for one thing we should censor a good deal of the Old Testament before putting it into our children's hands – a great many of the episodes are not fit for children to read. And, for another thing, it is difficult for children to pick out, by themselves, the stories likely to interest them. Some of the language is too difficult, and, in some instances, the story is rather involved. It was a pleasure to me to choose the tales, and to retell them simply and in a straightforward manner, keeping as closely as I could to the Old Testament narratives.

November, 1943   E.B.

Contents

1

The Beginning of the World

Long long ago, in the very beginning, the Lord God made the heaven and the earth. Into his mind came the thought of a fair and lovely world, and he began to make it.

At first all was darkness and confusion, and there was no day and no night.

Then God said, 'Let there be light.' And there was light. God saw the light, and knew that it was good. He divided the light from the darkness, and he called the light Day and the darkness Night.

Great waters covered the earth. God divided them, and made the dry land appear. There were seas, and sky and land, and light over everything. Great mountains towered up. Bare plains stretched for miles. It was a strange world, with nothing living in it, not even a blade of grass.

Then God commanded the grass to grow, and the plants and the trees, each with their own seed so that they might cover the earth with their green leaves and their beauty. And they grew so that they clothed the earth, and God saw that it was good.

Then, in the heaven above, so that the days and nights should follow one another, and the seasons of the year, God set the sun and the moon.

'Let them divide the day and the night, and let them be for signs and for seasons, and for days and for years,' said God. 'And let them give light upon the earth.'

And it was so. The sun shone in the day-time and gave light wherever its beams fell, and the moon shone at night, its silvery rays lighting up the tall mountains and the grass-covered plains. And God saw that it was good.

He set the stars in the heavens also, and the planets that move round the sun even as our world does.

The earth was silent except for the wind that moved the trees and whispered in the grass, and the waters that heaved and splashed. No bird flew in the air and called or sang. No animal pattered over the grass, or crept through the trees. There was no living creature on the earth.

Then the Lord God said: 'Let the waters bring forth in great numbers moving creatures that have life. Let there be winged birds that may fly above the earth in the wide skies.'

And in the waters came many living creatures, both small and great. There were fishes of all kinds, and there were great whales and other creatures. The air was full of sweet-voiced birds, whose wings took them over land and sea.

The Lord God made the animals too that walked on the face of the earth. He made the mighty ones whose feet shook the ground, and he made creatures so small that even a blade of grass would not bend beneath their weight. He made the gorgeous butterfly on the flower, and the hurrying beetle in the grass. He made the fierce tiger and the gentle lamb, the eagle soaring over the mountains, and the little robin in the hedge. Out of his great power and love he made them all, creating them in the long long days millions of years ago.

God looked on all that he had made and saw that it was good. He blessed it and commanded it to grow, and increase, so that always the earth might be filled with the creatures he had made. The flowers bore seed that became new plants. The birds laid eggs that became new nestlings, ready to fly when their wings were strong. The animals bore little ones that grew big, and, in their turn, became parents.

And last of all God made man. He made him in his own image and breathed life into him. He gave him the power to think, and he made him lord of all the creatures of the earth.

He called the man Adam, and he made a wonderful garden for him. Here, in this glorious garden, the Lord God planned that Adam should have peace and happiness without end, rejoicing in the beauty around him, talking with his God in the cool of the evening.

2

The Wonderful Garden

Every flower and tree grew and blossomed in the garden which the Lord God made for Adam. It was called the Garden of Eden, and never has there been such a beautiful place as this, that God made for the first man.

Flowers and fruit grew there, scenting the air all day long. A river flowed through the garden, and in it swam gleaming fishes. Birds sang in the trees, and flashed their bright wings in the sunshine. In the evening the dew fell, watering the garden so that it smelt sweet and fresh.

Adam was happy in the wonderful garden. He saw how beautiful it was. He heard the birds singing. He smelt the scent of the flowers, and he picked the ripe fruits. The sun warmed him, and he was glad to be alive.

Animals of all kinds lived with Adam in the garden. They lived at peace with one another, and Adam was not afraid of them, for he did not know fear. He only knew happiness and content. The wild beasts came to him in friendliness, and he gave them names. God made him lord of them all.

God spoke to Adam in love and kindness. 'Behold, all these things I have made are yours to love and enjoy. Do with them as you wish. There is food for you on the trees, ripe and sweet. Pluck it and eat it.

'But do not pluck the fruit of the Tree that grows

in the midst of the Garden. This Tree is the Tree of Knowledge of Good and Evil, and the fruit is not for you. If you should eat it, then your happiness will go, and your life of gladness and content will end. The fruit of this Tree is deadly, and may not be touched.'

Adam listened to God, and did not eat from the strange Tree which grew in the midst of the Garden. Day by day went by, and Adam lived happily in Eden, watching the birds flying above him, and the animals playing and feeding all around. He watched the birds drinking from the river, lifting their heads to let the water trickle down their beaks. He saw the animals lying in the warm sunshine, and watched them running swiftly, leaping in the air, happy in their strength and beauty.

In the cool of the evening God talked with Adam, and knew his thoughts. So, when Adam was lonely, and wished that he might have someone like himself to live with and love, God read his thoughts.

'It is not good that the man should be alone,' God said. 'I will make him a companion.'

Then, whilst Adam was in a deep sleep, God made a woman. He breathed life into her, and she lay beside Adam, in the darkness of the night, sleeping.

Morning came, and the sun lay golden over the Garden. The birds awoke and sang, calling to one another in the sweetness of the morning. The animals awoke too, and leapt to their feet, glad that day had come again.

Then Adam awoke, and opened his eyes. He saw the woman asleep beside him, and she was fair and sweet. He had never before seen one of his own kind, and now, here was a dear companion for him.

He touched her and she awoke. They looked at one another, and love came into their hearts. Adam longed to cherish and protect this gentle companion, and Eve, the woman, longed to follow Adam where he went and love him dearly.

Adam loved Eve, his wife. He showed her all the beauties of the Garden, and it was his greatest pleasure to see her happiness in the birds and flowers around. She soon knew the birds and animals as he did, and they wandered together in the Garden, full of happiness and delight.

They came to the mysterious Tree – the Tree of the Knowledge of Good and Evil. Its ripe fruits shone on its branches. Eve stretched out her hand to take some.

'We must not eat the fruit of this Tree,' said Adam. 'Come away. The Lord God has forbidden us to taste the sweetness of the fruit that grows on the Tree of Knowledge of Good and Evil.'

3
Eve and the Serpent

Now, of all the beasts in the Garden of Eden, the serpent was the most cunning. He coiled himself among the trees, watching Adam and Eve, seeing their happiness. He saw them eat the fruit of the trees, but he noticed that never did they eat of the fruit of the Tree that grew in the midst of the garden.

One day Eve was alone. Adam had gone to bathe in the river, and Eve sat in the sushine, waiting for him. She idly picked a ripe fruit from the tree nearby, and bit into it.

The serpent uncoiled his long, shining body and slid near to Eve. She was not afraid of him for neither she nor Adam had any fear of the animals and birds in the garden.

'The fruit from the trees is good,' said the wily serpent, and he raised his flat head to look at Eve. 'But why do you not eat the most delicious fruit of all? I have never seen you or Adam pick it, and yet it is the best in the garden.'

'What fruit is that?' asked Eve, in wonder.

'It is the fruit of the Tree of Knowledge of Good and Evil,' said the serpent. 'It grows nearby in the midst of the Garden, and its fruit is ripe and sweet now. Why do you not taste it, Eve?'

'I must not,' said Eve. 'Adam told me it was forbidden.'

'Who forbade it?' asked the serpent.

'The Lord God himself,' said Eve.

'But why must you not eat it?' asked the serpent. 'It is the sweetest fruit in the Garden. It will do you no harm.'

'We must not eat it because our happiness would go, and our life of gladness would end,' said Eve.

'Do not believe it!' said the cunning serpent. 'There is but one reason and one reason only why God has forbidden you to taste the fruit – and the reason is that once you have tasted the fruit of the Tree of Knowledge, you will know both good and evil, which God only and his holy angels know. You would be as powerful as God himself, and this he does not want.'

Eve listened in wonder, looking at the unblinking eyes of the strange serpent. She gazed across the glade at the Tree of Knowledge.

Glowing fruit hung from the branches. It looked more delicious than any Eve had ever tasted. The boughs were weighed down with the strange fruit, which shone deliciously in the bright sun. There could be no harm in looking at it.

Eve arose and went to the mysterious Tree. She stood and gazed at the laden branches. The serpent slid beside her, his little eyes gleaming.

'Would you not like to be as powerful and as wise as God himself?' asked the serpent. 'Is not this Tree the very one that the Lord God eats from? Why should not you too taste the wonderful fruit?'

Eve stretched out her hand and felt the softness of the ripe fruit on the Tree. She plucked it and smelt its sweetness. Then, quite unable to stop herself, she bit into it, and tasted the sweet, strong juice.

The fruit of the Tree was strange to eat. Eve

16

Eve stretched out her hand and felt the softness of the ripe fruit on the tree

plucked another and ran to find Adam. She met him coming from the river, and pressed it into his hand.

'Eat!' she said, and he ate the fruit too. And then they were both ashamed and unhappy, for they knew they had done wrong, and had disobeyed the Lord their God. He had given them so much that was good and beautiful – and they had done the one thing he had commanded them not to do.

Now God came into the Garden in the evening to talk to the man and woman he had made. Adam and Eve heard him there, as the birds sang their last songs, and the sun sank in the golden clouds behind the trees.

But they did not go gladly to meet him as they usually did. They hid from him, ashamed and troubled. They had never felt fear or shame before, but now they did, and they could not understand it. They had eaten from the Tree of Knowledge, and now knew not only good but evil. Just as the knowledge of good brought them peace and happiness, so did the knowledge of evil bring them misery and shame.

God's voice came on the evening air.

'Adam! Where are you?'

Adam and Eve trembled. They had never before been afraid of meeting God, but now they hardly dared to come out from their hiding-place. They crept out of the bushes and, with their heads hanging, they came before God.

'I heard your voice in the garden, and I was afraid,' said Adam. 'I was ashamed, and I hid myself.'

God knew that Adam could not know shame or fear

if he had not eaten the fruit of the Forbidden Tree. He spoke sadly and sternly to Adam.

'How is it that you feel shame and fear? Have you eaten of the fruit of the Tree which I commanded you not to touch?'

Adam could not look at the Lord God. He answered in a low voice. 'It was the woman you gave to me who tempted me to eat the fruit,' he said. 'She gave it to me and I did eat.'

Eve wept bitterly. God turned to her and spoke. 'What is this that you have done?' he asked.

'The serpent tempted me, and I did eat of the fruit,' said Eve.

Then God turned to the serpent. 'Because of this thing you have done, your punishment shall be that always you shall crawl along the ground and shall never be able to lift yourself up.'

The serpent went away. Adam and Eve gazed fearfully at the Lord God. He was grieved and angry. The man and woman he had made could no longer be happy in the wonderful Garden, for they knew evil now as well as good.

'You too must be punished,' he said. 'You must leave this Garden I have made for you, and you must go out into the wide world beyond and work. You will know pain and sorrow and sickness, for these things come with a knowledge of evil. You must tend the ground, and grow food to eat. The peace and happiness of the Garden are no longer yours. The day will come when you will die, for death comes to those who eat of the Forbidden Tree.'

Adam and Eve were sad and afraid. They fled away to hide. God watched them go, grieved and stern.

They must leave the Garden for ever, and never return. The man and the woman he had made must live and work, and learn many hard lessons because of their disobedience.

God set angels of heaven, called Cherubim, at the gate of the Garden, and in their hands were flaming swords that turned every way. Never again did Adam and Eve enter the Wonderful Garden.

4
The Terrible Flood

Many hundreds of years went by, and the world was filled with great numbers of men and women. Some lived a life of hunting and wandering, pitching their tents at night, and riding onwards in the morning. Others made their homes on good ground, which they tended, and kept great herds of fat cattle, and flocks of fine sheep.

Yet others built great cities and lived there. Men became wise and clever, using their minds and their hands in all kinds of ways.

Adam and Eve had eaten the fruit of the Tree of Knowledge of Good and Evil; and all the men and women who came after them knew good and evil too. They could choose between the good and the bad, and, as the years went by, more and more chose the evil.

Cruelty and greed, hatred and violence ruled the earth. The Lord God looked down upon the world, and his heart was full of anger and sorrow. He saw evil everywhere, and very little good.

'I am sorrowful because I created the world, and because I made man,' said God. 'I see evil on the earth where I planned to see good and happiness. I have it in my heart to destroy man, and to do away with everything that has life, for I am sorry I created it.'

One man only did God see to be good and faithful. He was called Noah, and he lived apart from the wicked men of his time. He chose to do good instead of evil, and God did not want to destroy anything that was good.

He went to Noah and told him many terrible things. 'The end of the world is to come, for the earth is full of wickedness which must be destroyed. A great flood of water will cover the earth, but you and your family shall be saved.'

Noah listened in wonder to all that the Lord God told him. How was he to be saved from the great and terrible flood?

'Make yourself an ark, a ship of gopher wood,' commanded God. 'Make rooms within it, and daub it with pitch both within and without, so that no water can enter, and no rain beat in from above.'

Then God told Noah exactly how he was to make the ark, and Noah listened well. He called his three sons to him, Shem, Ham and Japheth, and they went out to cut down the trees out of which the great ship was to be made.

For weeks and months Noah and his family sawed and hammered, making the great ark that God had commanded. It was three storeys high, and had a door in the side and a long, narrow window near the roof. It was made of good hard wood, and inside were many rooms. Ladders led upwards through openings into the rooms above.

Noah daubed the outside of the great ship with pitch, and the inside also. For months the work went on, and the enormous ark rose high, casting a great shadow over the ground.

Passers-by came to look at it. They had never seen

a ship built on dry land before. They gazed at it in wonder and mockery.

'Why do you build this ship?' they asked.

'Because soon the Lord God will punish men for their wickedness, and will send a flood to drown the earth,' Noah answered. 'I and my family will be saved, for we shall enter this ark, and float upon the waters.'

Then the passing hunters or soldiers would laugh loudly, and jeer at Noah.

'He is mad! What flood could destroy the earth?'

The ark was very big, far bigger than Noah and his family would need. But God had planned the big ship for other creatures besides man. Into the ark with him Noah was to take two of every kind of living creature.

And so, before the floods began, Noah called to him two of every animal, bird or insect, two of every living creature, both male and female. Then, when God warned him that the time of destruction was come, Noah opened the great door of the ark, and he and his sons led the living creatures of the earth into the ark, two by two, until they were all in safety together. Food he took into the ark as well, for he had to feed not only his own family, but all the living creatures also.

The Lord God spoke to Noah, and promised that he would keep them alive and safe throughout the terrible days to come. Then into the ark, after all the creatures had entered in safety, went Noah, his three sons, Shem, Ham and Japheth, their wives and their children.

For days the weather had been strange and the skies had been dark. Great winds blew, and dust swept over the plains. Now the time had come for the skies to open, and the water to flood the world.

Noah shut the great door of the ark. It was dark inside, for there was no window save for the one near the roof. The living creatures in the ark, both man and beast, listened to the gale that blew outside. It grew bigger and louder, it roared and bellowed, and even the sturdy ark shook to the power of the wind.

The lightning flared in the sky and tore the heavy clouds in two. Everyone left on the earth was afraid. Only Noah and his family were not afraid. They had chosen good, and God had promised to save them. Only the wicked would be destroyed.

Then there came a pattering on the roof of the ark – the first heavy drops of rain.

'The windows of heaven have opened,' said Noah, as the rain grew louder and fiercer. Never before had such a deluge of water fallen upon the earth. The streams swelled into rivers, the rivers into torrents, and everywhere water swirled and rushed.

Hour after hour the rain beat down upon the ark. Soon it was afloat, for the floods had now begun upon the earth. Noah and his family felt the great ship move and shake. She was sailing upon the waters.

Water surged against the strong wooden sides of the ark. A steady roar of rain was the only thing that could be heard. Noah looked from the long window, and in the lightning flashes saw a strange and terrible world of heaving, restless water. Not a living thing was to be seen. Everything was lost in the terrible flood.

The ark floated on the waters. The rain fell without ceasing and the floods grew deeper and deeper. At first those within the ark were troubled and dismayed by the fearfulness of the storms, and the violence of the rain, but as the days went by, and the ark floated in safety, they grew peaceful and calm. There were many tasks to be done, and Noah and his family went about them steadily.

They fed the animals and tended them. They made sure that no water was leaking into the ark at any place. They often looked from the big window to see if there was any sign of the storm abating. But day after day and night after night the rains went on.

The waters grew deeper. The winds made waves on the terrible flood, and the ark swayed as it floated. It went where wind and water took it. There was nothing to be seen but grey mists, grey water and grey rain.

For forty days and forty nights the rain poured down. And then those in the ark lifted their heads to listen to the rain and the wind.

'The wind no longer blows so violently,' said Noah. 'The rain falls more lightly.'

It was true. The pattering noise became gentle instead of fierce, as the clouds thinned above. Noah looked out from the window, and saw that although everything around was misty, and nothing could be seen except the grey water around the ark, there was light in the sky once more. The sun would soon be out, and the mists would go.

There was great rejoicing in the ark. The birds sang softly and spread their wings, knowing that one day soon they would be able to fly once more. The animals stirred restlessly. The children were glad and excited.

There was no land to be seen from the window of the ark, for even the highest hills and mountains were covered by the water. The flood looked like an endless sea, heaving and tossing.

And then, at last, the mists cleared, and the bright sun shone down. The water turned to blue in the distance and the ark steamed in the warm rays of the sun. All the living creatures within it knew that the sun was out again, and a great joyfulness ran from end to end of the ark.

A warm wind blew over the waters. The ark swayed gently as it floated. The waters began to go down a little, but still there was no sign of land.

But at last, in the distance, a mountain-top was uncovered and gleamed in the sun. Then, with a slight jolt, the ark came to rest on the peak of the high mountain called Ararat. Noah and his family knew for certain then that the waters were going down. They saw the tops of other mountains, and longed for the time to come when the face of the earth might once more be seen.

Then Noah took a raven. He opened the window of the ark, and set the great black bird loose. In joy it spread its wings and flew strongly out over the waters in the sunshine. It did not come back to the ark, but took care of itself, its strong wings taking it to and fro over the waters.

Then Noah took a soft grey dove to the window and set her free. She clapped her wings together and flew gladly over the blue waters. But she came back to the ark, for she could not find anywhere to rest the sole of her foot.

Her cooing was heard, and Noah went to the window to let in the dove. He stretched out his hand and the dove flew down to him, her feet closing over

Noah waited a week, then he sent the dove forth again

his finger. He drew her into the ark, knowing that there could not be very much land showing yet, or she would not have returned.

Noah waited a week, and then he sent the dove forth again. She flew out gladly over the waters. In the evening she was cooing outside the ark once more, and Noah let her in. But this time she carried an olive leaf in her beak, and Noah rejoiced to see it.

He took the tender young leaf to show his family. 'A leaf from the olive tree!' he said. 'Now, indeed, we know that the water is low, for the tops of the trees must be showing above the surface!'

A week again went by and Noah let the dove free once more. She flew out, and this time she did not come back. The earth was free of the terrible floods.

Then Noah and his sons took off the roof of the great ark. Soon God spoke to him, and Noah rejoiced to hear his words.

'Go forth out of the ark,' said the Lord God. 'Take with you your wife, your sons, your sons' wives, and their children. Take also every living thing that is with you, beast and bird and creeping thing, so that they may be fruitful and multiply, bringing forth their children so that once more the earth will have its living creatures.'

Then Noah, with all his family, and with all the living creatures, went forth out of the ark, rejoicing greatly. They were glad to leave the ark, and they looked back in wonder at the big dark ship whose sides and bottom were now green and brown with many weeds.

The birds flew off gladly. The animals leapt and ran

in joy, glad to see once more the green valleys and hills. The children shouted and ran about.

Then Noah built an altar, a place where he might worship God and pray to him, thanking him for bringing him and his family to safety.

Then God's voice came to Noah, and he made him a solemn promise.

'I will never again destroy the earth and its living creatures, but, whilst the earth remains, seed-time and harvest, cold and heat, summer and winter, and day and night shall not cease. There shall never again come a great flood to cover the earth. And, as a token of my promise I will set a bow in the clouds, so that all who see it may remember my words.'

Then, as Noah and his family heard these words, a wonderful thing happened. A great arching bow appeared in the clouds opposite the sun, a bow made up of all the colours there are. It shone there, gleaming brilliantly, a thing of wonder and beauty.

It was the rainbow. Sometimes we see it in the clouds now, and when we do we can remember the promise that God made to Noah so many, many years ago.

5

The Boy With the Coloured Coat

There was once a great shepherd-prince called Jacob. He had thousands of fine cattle, and so many sheep that it was impossible to number them.

Jacob did not live in a city, but in wide tents that sheltered him, his family and his servants – tents that were pitched on grassy lands, in green valleys or on sunny hillsides.

When the flocks and the herds had eaten the juicy grass, the rich shepherd-prince took down his tents and moved somewhere else, where his animals might have fresh pasture. Jacob wandered hundreds of miles in his lifetime, and he had many sons who helped him in the work of guarding and tending the cattle and sheep.

Two sons he had whom he loved above all the others. They were the two youngest, Joseph and Benjamin. Joseph was a strong youth, but Benjamin was only a small child. Joseph loved him and played with him when he had time.

Jacob loved Joseph so much because he was the son of his favourite wife, and because Joseph was clever and kind. Jacob could not help showing that the young Joseph was his favourite, and he spoke to him lovingly, and gave him many presents.

The elder brothers were jealous of Joseph and hated him, all but the eldest, Reuben, who liked the lad. Joseph had many cruel words spoken to him by his other brothers, and they would not be friendly to him. If he had not had Reuben's smile, and his little brother Benjamin to love, the growing boy would have been very unhappy.

Now one day Jacob gave his favourite son a present. It was a wonderful coat, bright as a rainbow in its many colours. It was a long tunic with sleeves down to the wrist, gaily embroidered and beautiful in every way. Joseph was delighted with it.

He put it on, and walked among the hills in it, showing it to anyone he met. It suited the tall, strong boy well, and he looked like a young prince as he walked the hills, with his gay coat shining.

His ten elder brothers, who were watching the flocks and the herds, saw the boy coming and gazed in amazement and envy at the bright-coloured coat he wore.

'Who gave you that coat?' they demanded.

'Our father gave it to me,' answered Joseph.

The brothers talked angrily among themselves and would not admire the coat. 'Our father shows his love for this boy more and more,' they said. 'He favours him far above us. It is plain to see that when our father dies he will leave to Joseph more than he will leave to us. He means to make this boy a mighty prince. Always he favours him.'

Of all the presents that Jacob gave to Joseph, the coat of many colours angered the ten brothers most bitterly. They hated to see the boy wearing it, and they scorned him and spoke spitefully to him.

There was another thing that the brothers disliked about Joseph, too, and this was his strange dreams. The boy had always had queer dreams so vivid that they seemed quite real to him. He could tell them to the others like a story, forgetting nothing.

'When *we* have dreams, they are past and gone like a mist when we awake,' grumbled the brothers. 'But Joseph sits and tells us his dreams as if they really happened.'

'Maybe his dreams have a meaning,' said Reuben.

Now, one summer's day, when the harvest was being gathered in, and all the brothers were working hard together, Joseph was rather silent. He had had a queer dream the night before, and it had been so real that he had kept remembering it. His brothers had found much fault with him in the harvesting, and the dream had comforted him.

'What is the matter?' asked Reuben, seeing that Joseph was lost in thought.

'I had a strange dream last night,' said Joseph. The others looked up, for they knew Joseph's queer dreams and wondered what this one had been.

'What was your dream?' they asked.

Then Joseph told them. 'Hear my dream,' he said. 'Behold, I thought we were all binding sheaves together in the field, even as we have been doing for days. I bound my sheaf of corn and laid it down. You, my brothers, also bound your sheaves and laid them down, And then, even as I looked, my sheaf suddenly rose up, and stood by itself! And then all your sheaves rose up, and stood.

'But that was not all. Your sheaves suddenly bowed themselves down to my sheaf, as if they were servants bowing to their master. It was indeed a strange sight. I cannot forget this dream. It is in my mind all the time.'

His brothers heard this dream in anger. They hardly waited to hear the end before they shouted loudly at Joseph.

'You need not ask us the meaning of your dream!' they cried. 'You are trying to pretend that we bowed down to you! Who are you that you should be greater than we? Do you really think you are going to reign over us?'

And the brothers hated Joseph even more for his dream. They could not help thinking that their young brother's dreams *did* have a meaning, and it angered them.

Then Joseph dreamed another dream, and again he told it to the others, and to his father, too.

'Behold!' said Joseph, 'I have dreamed yet again, and it is an even stranger dream. I thought I was in the sky, and, lo, the sun and the moon and eleven stars all bowed down before me.'

The brothers looked at one another sneeringly. They knew that in the dream they and Benjamin were the eleven stars, and they were angry. Joseph's father was angry also.

'What is this dream that you have dreamed?' said Jacob sternly. 'Do you really think that I and your mother and your eleven brothers will bow ourselves down to the earth before you?'

But although his father spoke sternly to his favourite son, he remembered the dream and puzzled over it. He watched Joseph, and thought him to be a strange and unusual boy. His brothers envied him, and lost no chance of being scornful and unkind. They jeered at the two dreams – but there came a day when they remembered them again in astonishment and wonder.

His brothers heard this dream in anger

6
The Unkind Brothers

Now one day Jacob sent the ten elder brothers to the beautiful valley of Shechem, where there was much green grass for the flocks and herds. They set off with their sheep and cattle, their dogs helping them to lead the flocks. When they came to the valley, which was a good many miles away, they pitched their tents and prepared to stay there for some time.

Jacob had no word from the brothers, and he wondered if they were safe and well. So he called Joseph to him, and spoke to the handsome seventeen-year-old boy.

'Joseph, your brothers are feeding the flocks in Shechem. I have a mind to send you to them.'

Joseph was glad. He felt a man to be sent on such a long journey by himself. 'Here I am,' he said joyfully. 'Send me.'

'You shall go and see whether all is well with your brothers and with the flocks,' said Jacob. 'Find them and speak with them, then bring me word.'

Joseph took a camel to ride, and in the baskets slung at each side were presents of food for his ten elder brothers. He took them wine to drink, and oil, and dried raisins and he was happy and excited as he set off alone to ride the many miles to Shechem.

He rode for some time – but when he came to Shechem Valley there was no sign of tents or flocks. The boy was surprised, and wandered about for a good time, trying to find his brothers. A stranger met him and told him where they were.

Joseph set off on his camel once more, glad to hear that his brothers were well, and only had moved their flocks because they had heard of a better pasture for them. He hastened on his way, thinking joyfully how pleased his brothers would be to see him, how glad they would be to have his presents, and how surprised that he had been able to find his way to them all alone.

The ten brothers were sitting with their flocks. Most of them were very much older than Joseph, and were strong, bearded men, with wives and children of their own. They suddenly saw the lone camel coming towards them, and sat up to see who was the rider.

They saw that it was Joseph, in his coat of many colours. They sat and looked at the coming rider with hate and jealousy in their hearts. They had no welcome for him.

'Behold! The dreamer comes!' they said to one another mockingly.

Then, when they saw that he was quite alone, a wicked plan came into their minds.

'Let us kill him,' they said. 'We will throw him into a pit, and say that some wild beast has eaten him. We will see what becomes of his wonderful dreams then!'

Reuben, the eldest brother, heard what they were saying. He was uneasy, for he did not hate Joseph as the others did. He knew also that Jacob, his father, loved Joseph with all his heart, and would be bitterly grieved if the boy died.

'No, no,' said Reuben. 'We must shed no blood. Is he not our brother? Cast him into a pit if you will, but do not kill him.'

Reuben meant to go to the pit that night and take Joseph out to send him back unhurt to his father. But he did not tell the other brothers this, for he thought that if he did they would surely kill Joseph.

So whilst Joseph rode eagerly towards them on his camel the brothers argued whether or not they should kill him; at last they decided they would not, but would cast him into a pit, where he could die of hunger and thirst.

Joseph drew near on his camel. He waved to his brothers, thinking that they would come to greet him. But they did not. Instead they looked at him with hatred and scorn. He leapt off his camel as soon as it knelt down and ran to greet his brothers, crying out that he had brought presents for them.

But they would not kiss him or welcome him. Reuben, who might have been kind, was no longer there, for he had had to leave the brothers to see to the flocks. So Joseph faced nine stern-faced men as he ran up.

They took hold of him roughly. They stripped off his coat of many colours. They bound him hand and foot and threw him into a pit, rolling a big stone over the mouth. Then they went to find the presents the boy had brought, and soon they were sitting down eating the raisins and figs and drinking the wine.

Joseph was astonished and horrified. He knew that his brothers disliked him, but he had never thought they would treat him in such a cruel way. He lay in the pit, listening to them talking and laughing. He was bruised and unhappy, and he was afraid of what might happen to him. Were his brothers going to kill him? Where was Reuben? Surely he would save him?

Now, as the nine brothers sat eating, they saw in the distance a company of desert traders on their camels. The shepherds often saw these men, and talked to them as they passed. They were fierce men, trading over the desert, travelling great distances on their camels. They took spicery and balm and myrrh, sweet-smelling and rare, down the desert tracks into Egypt, and brought back with them cotton and silk.

Sometimes, too, they bought and sold children as slaves. Often they took small black boys and girls away from their fathers and mothers, and sold them to Egyptian masters and mistresses. As soon as the nine brothers saw these desert traders on their camels an idea came to them.

It was the brother called Judah who spoke their thoughts aloud.

'What do we gain if we kill our brother Joseph?' he said. 'Even if we leave him here in the pit to die we shall be as guilty of his death as if we had killed him with our hands. But if we sell him as a slave to the traders we shall not only get rid of him, but we shall make a little money for ourselves also!'

Not one of the nine brothers said no to this horrible plan. They hailed the traders, who came up to them on their camels.

'We have a young boy here whom we will sell to you as a slave,' said Judah.

'Let us see him,' said the fierce traders.

Joseph was dragged out of the pit and unbound. He stood trembling there in the evening light, dazed and miserable, looking round in vain for Reuben. He heard his brothers bargaining for money with the traders, and he suddenly knew that they were selling him as a slave.

They did not listen to his cries and entreaties. They gave him to the traders for twenty pieces of silver. They stood and divided the money among themselves as the rough desert traders tied the boy's wrists to a camel's saddle and set off down the track with him.

Stumbling over the desert, pulled along by the camel, Joseph left his brothers behind. He turned to see the last of them, hoping that perhaps one of them might save him. He begged the dark-faced traders to take him back, but they paid no heed to his cries. They were used to buying and selling children, and to them he was simply a handsome young slave who would bring them much money. He was a Hebrew, and not a black-faced negro, so he would fetch more money.

Now that night Reuben went back to the camp. He crept to the pit to take out his young brother and send him back to his father. But the pit was empty.

Reuben thought that his brothers had killed him. He was filled with horror and dismay. He tore his clothes in despair and went to his brothers.

'The boy is gone?' he said. 'And now what shall I do?'

The brothers did not tell Reuben what had happened. They took the coat of many colours and dipped it into the blood of a kid belonging to some goats they had. The blood stained the gay coat, so that it seemed as if the wearer must have fallen into danger and been killed.

The next day the brothers took their flocks and went homewards to where their father lived. They came before him, and he looked eagerly to see if Joseph was with them. But he was not.

'See what we have found,' said the brothers. 'Is it Joseph's coat?'

Jacob looked at the blood-stained coat in sorrow and despair, for he knew that it was the coat that he himself had given to Joseph.

'It is my son's coat,' he said, weeping. 'An evil beast has eaten him. Without doubt Joseph has been torn to pieces.'

7

The Slave-boy Joseph

Whilst Jacob was so bitterly weeping for Joseph, whom he thought dead, the boy was being taken to Egypt. The journey took many days, but at last the boy came to the chief city of Egypt, and saw many sights that were new and strange to him. He was used to living in tents, with wide-spreading plains and valleys around him, but now he saw great houses, and more people gathered together in one place than he had ever seen in his life before.

Joseph was taken to be sold in the slave-market. He stood there with other boys and girls, waiting for someone to buy him. He looked a fine boy, for he was strong and handsome, and his eyes were keen and fearless.

Potiphar, a rich Egyptian and an officer of Pharaoh, the king of Egypt, saw the boy and stopped to look at him. He needed a slave for himself, and he liked the look of Joseph. He bought him and took him back to his house with him.

Potiphar lived in a lovely house with magnificent gardens, and farms that supplied much of the food that was needed. At first Joseph felt strange in such a place, for he had never lived under a roof before, but only in a great tent. But soon he knew every inch of Potiphar's house and garden, and his keen mind soon understood how it was run, and all that was done there.

Joseph was a clever and honest youth. Whatever he did he did well, and Potiphar liked him and trusted him. He soon found that the slave-boy was far wiser and cleverer than any of his servants, and, what was more, could always be trusted in even the smallest thing.

So as the time went by and the boy grew into a young man, Potiphar put more and more into his hands. He gave him charge of his goods, and his money. He put him in charge of his household, and allowed him to oversee everything. Before many years had passed Joseph was the head of the house, under Potiphar, and when his master was away the young man saw to everything, buying and selling, guarding his master's money and goods as if they were his own.

Potiphar used to boast of his clever slave. 'I know nothing of what goes on in my household – I see what is put before me to eat and drink, but that is all I trouble to know!' said Potiphar. 'Joseph, my slave, manages everything for me, and since he came to me my whole household has been happy and has prospered well.'

But the day came when Joseph had to leave Potiphar's house. Potiphar's wife took a dislike to the young man, and spoke evil of him to her husband. Potiphar believed her, and, in disgust at what he thought was the young man's deceit, he had him thrown into prison.

But, even in prison, the young man's clever brain and complete honesty served him well. The guards saw that he was a good and pleasant youth, and they stopped beating him and took off his chains.

They spoke well of him to the governor of the

prison, and said that Joseph was clever and much to be trusted. They told the governor of his quick brain and of how wise his advice always was.

And so it came about that even the governor of the prison trusted Joseph and soon put him in charge of all the other prisoners. And, as time went on, he even put him in charge of the prison itself, so that Joseph had only the governor over him. He did his work quickly and well, and everyone loved him and admired him, the lowest prisoner as well as the governor himself.

Now one day the governor called Joseph to him and spoke to him.

'Two new prisoners are to come today,' he said. 'One is the king's butler, he who fills his cup with wine for him, and the other is the king's baker, he who prepares his bread.'

'Why has Pharaoh sent them to prison?' asked Joseph in surprise. 'They are surely men of high rank. Have they been trying to poison the Pharaoh?'

'That I do not know,' answered the governor. 'The king himself is making inquiries, and if he finds the men are guilty, then he will set their punishment. But I have called you to me, Joseph, because I want to put you in charge of these two men. You will wait on them and serve them.'

So it came about that Joseph waited on the king's cup-bearer and on the king's baker. The two men, who were afraid of what might be going to happen to them, liked the young man very much. They talked to him and told him their troubles and their fears.

When some months had gone by these two men each dreamed a strange dream on the same night. The dreams were so real to them that each prisoner felt there must be some meaning or warning in his dream. They sat silently, puzzling over their dreams, and Joseph was surprised to see them both looking so sad.

'Why do you look so sad today?' the young man asked.

'We have each dreamed a strange dream,' they answered. 'And we are sad because we cannot go to anyone in the city who could tell us the meaning of our dreams.'

In those days the Egyptians thought that dreams had a meaning, and there were men who, for a sum of money, would tell them the meaning. The butler and the baker would dearly have loved to go to someone who would explain the dreams to them.

Joseph remembered the strange dreams he himself had had as a boy. 'I, too, have dreamed dreams,' he said. 'Tell me your dreams, I pray you.'

So the butler told his dream first. 'In my dream,' he said, 'behold a grape-vine was before me; it had three branches, and, even as I watched, it budded and broke into blossom. The blossoms became ripe grapes. Then I saw that I had Pharaoh's cup in my hand, and I took the grapes and pressed the juice into the cup for my master. I gave the cup into Pharaoh's hand that he might drink.'

Joseph listened closely to the dream. He stood, lost in thought, trying to find the meaning. Then he spoke to the butler.

'I know the meaning of your dream,' he said. 'The three branches of the vine are three days; and in three days shall Pharaoh send for you, and pardon you and

'I know the meaning of your dream,' he said

you shall give to him his cup of wine as you always did.'

The butler was overjoyed. Joseph saw his delight and spoke again to him. 'Think of me when all is well with you, and you are once more with your master, loved and trusted. Show kindness to me, and tell Pharaoh about me, so that I may be taken out of prison. I only became a slave because I was stolen away from my family, and I have done nothing in this land for which I should be put into prison.'

The butler gladly promised Joseph that he would remember him when he went back to Pharaoh. Then the baker begged the young man to explain his dream to him also.

'Tell me your dream,' said Joseph.

'This was my dream,' he said. 'Behold, I was walking along, and on my head I carried three white baskets. In the topmost basket there were all kinds of cakes for the king. As I walked along, the birds flew down and ate the cakes from the basket. What is the meaning of my dream?'

Joseph did not want to tell the baker the meaning of his dream. He knew at once what it was. But the man begged him to explain it, and at last Joseph told him.

'Alas,' he said, 'the three baskets in your dream are three days; in three days will Pharaoh send for you to punish you. You will be hanged, and the birds of the air will fly around your head.'

The baker was frightened to hear this. The three days went slowly by, and on the third day it was even as Joseph said.

Pharaoh's birthday came on the third day, and the

king gave a great feast to his servants. He had found out that his butler was not the rogue he had feared him to be, so he pardoned him and sent for him to hold his cup of wine once more. The man left the prison rejoicing, and gave the king his wine as he always used to do.

But the baker was guilty of wrong-doing and he was hanged.

Joseph hoped that the butler would remember him and speak of him to Pharaoh; but the man forgot about him, and so Joseph still remained in prison, trusted and liked, but unable to get his freedom.

8
The King's Strange Dreams

One night Pharaoh, ruler of Egypt, dreamed a queer dream. He awoke and thought about it. It had been so real and so clear that the king felt certain there was some strange warning in it.

He lay and thought of his dream. 'What did I dream? I dreamed that I stood beside the river, and as I stood there seven cows came out of the waters. They were beautiful cows, fat and good to see. And, behold, there came after them out of the river, seven other cows. But these were different. They were ugly and thin, and I shuddered to see them. And even as I looked I saw the thin cows eat up the fat cows. Then I awoke, and remembered my dream.'

Pharaoh fell asleep once more. He dreamed again, and awoke, fearful and puzzled. 'I have dreamed again,' he thought. 'This time in my dream I saw seven good ears of corn growing upon one stalk. Then came seven thin ears of corn, poor and bad, spoilt by the east wind. And, lo, the seven thin ears ate the seven fat ears. Now what can be the meaning of these two strange dreams?'

Pharaoh could not forget these dreams. He was worried and anxious. Had these dreams been sent to him to warn him of something? Why were there *seven* cows and *seven* ears of corn? Somehow he must find the meaning of the dreams.

So that morning Pharaoh sent for the chief wise

men of Egypt, and all his magicians. He could not help feeling that these dreams of his were important. He sat on his throne in a robe of gold and told the wise men his dreams.

They listened in silence, looking at one another to see if anyone knew the meaning. But not one of the men there understood what the dreams meant.

'What is the meaning of the two dreams?' demanded Pharaoh, and he looked at first one magician and then another. But each one shook his head.

Everyone in the place had heard of the king's strange dreams, and how even the wise men did not know what they meant. The king's butler knew of them too, and he saw that his master was troubled in his mind.

Then the butler suddenly remembered the young man in the prison, and tried to think of his name. He spoke eagerly to his master.

'Lord,' he said, 'I have just remembered something I should never have forgotten. In the days when you were angry with me and with the chief baker, and put us into prison, we both dreamed dreams one night. We were sorely troubled with these dreams, and we told them to a young man who was servant to the captain of the guard. He at once told us the meaning of our dreams. He said that my dream meant that you would forgive me and take me back, as you did; but that the baker would be hanged, as he was.'

'Where is the young man now?' asked Pharaoh.

'Lord, in prison still,' said the butler. 'I promised him I would remember him and speak to you of him so that he might have his freedom. But until this day I did not remember him.'

49

'Send for him,' commanded Pharaoh.

Then a messenger was sent to the governor of the prison, that Pharaoh wished to see his servant, Joseph. The governor was glad, for he liked and trusted Joseph. He sent for the young man, and allowed him to bathe himself and shave, and to put on good clothes so that he might appear before the king.

And so it came about that Joseph stood before the Pharaoh, and heard him speak.

'I have dreamed a dream,' said Pharaoh. 'And no one can explain it to me, no, not one of all these wise men and magicians you see before me. But I have heard it said of you that you know the meaning of dreams.'

'It is not I who gives the dreams, nor is it I who gives the meaning,' answered Joseph. 'It is God.'

And then Pharaoh told Joseph his two dreams – the one of the seven fat cows being eaten by the seven thin ones, and the second dream of the seven good ears of corn being eaten by the seven thin ones.

'Now tell me the meaning of these two dreams,' he commanded.

Joseph knew at once what the strange dreams meant.

'The two dreams are one,' he said. 'In these dreams God has shown Pharaoh what is about to happen. The seven good cows are seven years, and the seven good ears of corn are the same seven years. The seven thin cows that come after the seven good cows are also seven years, and the seven poor ears of corn are the same seven years. Both dreams are really one.

'Now, as I have said, God has shown to Pharaoh what is about to happen, and the meaning of the

Pharaoh listened in silence to the young man

dreams is this: Behold, there will come seven years of great plenty throughout all the land of Egypt. But after them shall come seven years of famine and terrible hunger, when there are no harvests, and the people starve. Then the seven years of plenty will be forgotten. The famine will be so terrible that God has warned Pharaoh twice in his dreams, so that he may surely know what is about to happen.'

Pharaoh listened in silence to the young man. He knew at once that the meaning was right, and all the wise men knew it too. The king's dreams had been a double warning.

Pharaoh thought over what Joseph had said. So there were to be seven good years of plenty, and then seven bad years. What would be the best thing to do? He spoke again to Joseph, thinking that as the young man had been wise enough to explain his dreams to him, he would also be clever enough to say what might be done for the best.

'What would your God have me do?' he said.

Joseph stood in thought. He was wise beyond his years, and his counsel was good.

'Let Pharaoh look out a man discreet and wise,' he said, 'and set him over the land of Egypt. Let Pharaoh do this, and let him appoint officers over the land who will take a fifth of the harvest of corn during the seven good years. Store this corn in great granaries, where it will keep until the seven bad years come. Then, when the famine is here, and the people hunger for food, and have none, open the granaries and sell them corn for bread.'

Pharaoh listened and marvelled at the good sense and wisdom of the young man. He had been amazed at the way Joseph had explained his dreams, and now was even more amazed at the simple and direct answer Joseph gave to the problem of the seven good and bad years. He turned to his wise men and his servants.

'Where could we find a man such as this one?' he said. 'The spirit of God is in him.'

Then he turned to Joseph and spoke gravely to him.

'If God has shown you all this, then there can be none in my kingdom wiser than you are. You shall be the man discreet and wise, whom I will put over all the land of Egypt. You shall be over my house, and you shall appoint the officers who will take up the fifth of the corn each year, to keep until the years of famine. No one in the land shall be greater than you, save only myself.'

Then Pharaoh took off his ring from his hand and put it upon Joseph's hand, and he gave him robes of fine linen such as only the chief lords wore, and put a chain of gold about his neck.

'See, I have set you over all the land of Egypt,' said Pharaoh.

Pharaoh also gave Joseph a wonderful chariot to ride in, second only in richness to his own. In this Joseph rode out over the land of Egypt, with a runner before him to announce his coming. He was second in the land, with only the king over him, Pharaoh's friend and counsellor, trusted beyond any other man.

Then came the seven years of plenty as the dreams had foretold. In these years the harvests were wonderful, and people marvelled at the abundance of corn. Joseph appointed a man in each district whose duty it was to take a fifth of all the corn that was harvested.

Great granaries were built in the cities, and much

corn was stored there. As the years of plenty went by, these enormous granaries, store-houses of grain, were filled to the roof, and at last there was so much corn in store that it could no longer be measured.

Joseph saw that his commands were obeyed and knew that there was a vast store of food hoarded in every city of Egypt. Then came the seventh and last year of plenty. Joseph took a fifth of the corn once more, and sealed up the granaries, for he knew that no more good harvests would come until the next seven years had passed.

And now came the seven years of famine. The harvests were bad everywhere, not only in Egypt, but in all the lands around. Year after year went by, and still the corn failed, and people began to starve. They soon ate what they had stored up themselves, and then they cried out to Pharaoh for bread.

'Go to Joseph, my counsellor,' said the king. 'What he says to you, do.'

Then Joseph, who saw that it was time to use his stores of corn, gave orders that the great granaries should be opened, and that the corn stored in them should be sold to any who wished to buy. He himself fixed the price of the corn, and soon Pharaoh's treasure-chamber was filled with money.

Not only did the Egyptians come to buy corn, but strangers from all the lands round about. For in these lands too the harvests failed, year after year, and the people were starving. The news spread from mouth to mouth that there was corn in Egypt, and men mounted their camels, their horses or their donkeys and made haste to go to Egypt to buy corn for their hungry families.

9
Joseph and His Brothers

Now, in the land of Canaan, where Jacob, Joseph's father, still lived with Benjamin, and with the rest of his sons, the famine was as great as in any other land. The years of hunger were terrible, and Jacob could not bear to see his family and his flocks with no corn to eat.

'There is corn in the land of Egypt,' said Jacob to his sons. 'Go there, and buy some for us.'

So the ten brothers mounted their camels, and, with a string of asses following to carry the corn they hoped to bring back, they set out for the faraway land of Egypt. They took the same track down which Joseph had been taken years before by the fierce desert-traders.

They came to the chief city of Egypt, and were amazed at the great numbers of people there. There were far more people in the city than usual because so many strangers had come from the lands round to buy corn.

The ten shepherd brothers were taken before the chief man of Egypt, second only to Pharaoh himself. This man was Joseph. He was no longer a boy, as he had been when his brothers sold him as a slave. He was a grown man, and he was dressed in the Egyptian way. He was shaved, unlike his brothers, who all wore beards. He wore a great wig of black horse-hair, and he was dressed in the finest of white linen, with Pharaoh's gold chain around his neck.

He had servants to wait on him. He had scribes, or writing-men, to write down all that was sold to the men who came for corn. He sat in his great hall, looking rich and grand and powerful.

The ten shepherds gazed in awe at this great man. They had no idea he was their own young brother. They stood before him, rough shepherds from the hills, waiting to ask him the favour of food for their hungry families.

Joseph glanced up. He saw the ten men, and in an instant he knew them at once. He saw Reuben – Judah – Simeon – and all the others he had once known so well. His own brothers!

He saw them with joy and gladness, but he did not show this. Though his heart turned over within him for gladness at seeing his family again, he had not forgotten that once they had been wicked. He meant to test them now, to see if they had changed, or were sorry for what they had once done to him.

So he gazed at them with a stern face and they trembled. They bowed themselves down before him – and Joseph suddenly remembered his dream of long ago.

'I dreamed that their sheaves of corn arose and bowed themselves down to mine,' he thought. 'And here is my dream come true. My brothers are bowing themselves down before me, begging for corn.'

Joseph wanted to know all about his family. He wanted to know if his father was still alive, and if little Benjamin, who must now be a young man, was also still alive. He questioned them roughly, pretending to be angry with them, so that he might frighten out of them what he longed to know, without their guessing who he was.

'Where do you come from? Who are you? How do I know that you are not spies?'

'We come from the land of Canaan to buy food,' answered the brothers, afraid. 'We are not spies. We are all sons of one man. We are twelve brothers. The youngest of all is with our father, for he would not let him come with us for fear that harm might come to him. And the twelfth brother is dead.'

Joseph was glad to hear that Jacob and Benjamin were alive. He longed to see Benjamin, and he spoke even more sternly to the ten brothers.

'Now, to prove to me that you are not spies, return home with the corn, and come back here to me with your brother Benjamin, that I may see if you speak truly to me. Leave one of your number here in prison, so that if you do not return, he may be punished for you.'

Then the brothers spoke among themselves in their own language, which was not the Egyptian language. They did not guess that Joseph, the great lord, understood every word they said!

'Now are we punished for the wrong we once did to our young brother Joseph,' they said. 'We showed him no mercy when he cried out for pity. We saw the fear and sadness in his eyes, but we took no heed. And now, as a punishment, this trouble has come upon us.'

Then Reuben spoke to the brothers. 'Did I not say to you "Do not hurt the child" and you would not listen to me?'

Joseph heard these words, and he was sad to see the brothers' distress and fear. He turned himself away from them to hide the tears in his eyes. He longed so much to see his father and Benjamin, and when he remembered the days of his boyhood he could not keep from weeping.

Joseph commanded the sacks the brothers had brought to be filled with corn. He also bade his servants to put into the mouth of each sack the money his brothers had given to pay for the corn. He took his brother Simeon and bound him in the sight of the others, saying that he was to remain behind until the brothers came again, bringing Benjamin with them.

The nine brothers were glad to be safely on their way home again. They came to Jacob, their father, and told him all that had happened.

'We must return to Egypt, and we must take Benjamin with us,' they said. 'Simeon we have had to leave behind. But see, we have brought much corn for our families and our flocks.'

They opened the sacks they had brought with them, and saw, to their amazement and fear, that each man's money was at the top of the sack. Then they were really afraid for they thought that when they returned to Egypt they might be accused of not paying for the corn.

'You shall not take my youngest and dearest son back with you,' said Jacob. 'Have I not lost Joseph? And shall I lose Benjamin too? No, you shall not take him.'

Now when Jacob and his family had eaten all the corn they had brought, famine was still in the land,

and it was terrible to see the people's hunger. Jacob spoke to his sons.

'Go again and buy us food.'

'Then we must take Benjamin,' said the brothers. 'Unless we do we shall get no corn.'

And so at last Jacob consented, and bade Judah take the greatest care of his youngest boy.

'Take presents for this great man,' said Jacob. 'And take double money, and also the money that was in the mouth of the sacks, in case it had been put there by mistake.'

Then once again the brothers went down to Egypt and this time they took Benjamin with them. He was a fine young man, and eager to see the great city of which his brothers had so often spoken.

They came to the great granary, and word was sent to Joseph that the Hebrew shepherds had again come to the city. He commanded that they should be taken to his house, and he would dine with them at noon.

So the ten brothers were taken to the beautiful house belonging to Joseph, and they marvelled at the lovely gardens, the wonderful terraces and brilliant flowers. They were surprised to be taken there, and afraid. They spoke to the steward of the house.

'When we returned home, we found our money in our sacks,' they said. 'It was not our fault. We have brought it back.'

'Do not fear,' said the steward. 'I myself know that you paid for your corn.'

Then Simeon, the brother who had been left behind, was brought to them. The servants gave them water to wash their dusty feet, and their asses were fed and tended.

Then Joseph came. The brothers took the presents they had brought, and bowed low before him. He stood and gazed at them, glad to see them all.

'Is your father well?' he asked. 'Is the old man still alive?'

They answered yes. Then Joseph saw Benjamin, and said happily, 'Is this your young brother?'

He looked long at his young brother, and said, in a voice that almost shook, 'God be gracious to you, my son!'

And then, because he could not keep back the tears of sudden gladness that came to his eyes, he turned swiftly and went to his room. He wept for joy to know that his father was alive, and that his beloved brother Benjamin was waiting to eat with him in the nearby room. He washed his face and went back to his brothers.

'Serve the meal,' he said to his servants and they put out the bread and the meat. Joseph seated his brothers according to their age, the eldest at the top, and the youngest at the foot, and all the brothers marvelled, wondering how he guessed their ages.

They feasted well, and were merry. Afterwards Joseph sent for his steward, and spoke secretly to him.

'Fill these men's sacks with food, as much as they can carry, and put every man's money back into his sack. And put my silver drinking-cup into the sack's mouth of the youngest brother, with his money.'

This was done, and in the morning the eleven brothers (for Simeon was now with them) went away. Then Joseph sent his steward after them, with servants.

'When you come upon the shepherd-brothers, say

to them, "How is it that you repay good with evil? Why have you taken the lord's own drinking-cup?"'

So the steward rode after the ten brothers and overtook them. He accused them of stealing Joseph's silver cup, and they were amazed and very frightened.

'Indeed, we are honest men,' said the brothers. 'We know nothing of the silver cup.'

'I will search your sacks,' said the steward. 'And he in whose sack I find the cup shall return with me to the city to be my lord's servant.'

And the steward searched all the sacks, beginning at Reuben's. The cup was in Benjamin's sack, and when it was taken out, all the brothers stared in horror. Then they tore their clothes in despair, loaded their donkeys again, and went back to the city as fast as they could. They came to Joseph, and flung themselves on the ground before him.

'I will only punish him in whose sack the cup was found,' said Joseph, who longed above everything to keep his brother Benjamin with him. 'The rest of you may return to your father.'

Then Judah, who had promised his father, Jacob, to take the greatest care of Benjamin, came forward and spoke with tears to Joseph.

'My father did not want this boy, his youngest son, to come with us,' said Judah. 'He had two favourite sons. One was killed and this other is left. If any harm comes to Benjamin, our youngest brother, the old man will surely die. So let me stay here as your servant instead of my father's best-beloved son. How can I go home to the old man and tell him such evil news?'

Joseph listened to Judah's pleading, and he could no longer keep his secret.

'Let everyone leave me except these shepherds!' he cried. And the Egyptians left the room in astonishment, seeing that Joseph was weeping. They heard his sobs as they stood outside the room.

His brothers looked at him, silent and fearful. 'I am Joseph, your brother!' said Joseph. 'Is my father still alive? Tell me truly.'

His brothers could not answer a word. They were afraid. This mighty lord of Egypt said and did strange things. How could he be their brother? Was he not an Egyptian?

'Come near to me. Look closely at me,' said Joseph. 'Can you not see that I am Joseph, your brother, whom you sold as a slave?'

Then, as the brothers looked closely at Joseph, they saw that he was indeed their own lost brother, and not a strange Egyptian. Joseph put his arms round them, one after another, still weeping for joy. He saw their fear and wonder, and knew that they might think he would be angry with them for what they had done to him as a boy. But he had forgiven them long since, and now he told them so.

'Be not grieved or angry that you sold me as a slave. God has sent me here to save your lives and many others in these terrible years of famine! I am lord of Pharaoh's house and a ruler of Egypt. So now make haste and go to tell my father all this, and bring him here, with all his family and flocks and herds. There are years of famine still to come, but I will give you a fair land to live in, and you shall have all you want.'

So, in great gladness of heart, the brothers returned to their old father, Jacob, and told him the strange and wonderful news.

'Joseph is still alive!' they said. 'He is governor over all the land of Egypt.'

Then Jacob almost fainted for joy, for he had never ceased loving his favourite son. He longed to see Joseph, and made ready to leave the land of Canaan, with all his family and flocks and herds.

And they went down into Egypt to Joseph, who welcomed them gladly, and was even happier to see his father than he had been to see Benjamin, his brother. He took Jacob to Pharaoh, and then he gave to his father's family the fair land of Goshen, where they might pasture their cattle and sheep and live happily together.

There they lived, looked after by Joseph, whilst the years of famine lasted. When they were over, the family of Jacob remained in Egypt, where their children grew up in great numbers, becoming rich and powerful men.

They were happy there, although they were strangers to the country, with different customs, and worshipped a god whom the Egyptians did not know. And because of this there came a time when great trouble fell upon them, and their friends were turned to foes.

10

The Baby in the Bulrushes

Now many years later, when Joseph was dead, a new Pharaoh ruled over Egypt. He cared nothing about Joseph and how he had saved the people from famine. He only saw that Joseph's family, the Hebrews, or, as they were often called, the Children of Israel (Jacob), were becoming very rich and powerful, and were overrunning the land.

He called a council and spoke gravely to his statesmen.

'Behold!' he said, 'these men are more and mightier than we are. We must deal sternly with them or it may be that one day, when we are at war, they will join our enemies and fight against us. We must put over them taskmasters, who will set them work to do, and who will give them no chance to rise up and fight against us.'

And so the Children of Israel were made into slaves for Pharaoh, and were given hard tasks to do by taskmasters set over them. They were made to build great treasure cities for Pharaoh, they were sent to cut wide canals and build dams.

They were forced to work in the blazing sun for long hours, with poor food to eat, and no wages for their work. Most of them worked in the river clay, making bricks. Some dug out the mud. Some trampled the clay with their feet or moulded it with their hands till it was soft enough to put into boxes that would shape the clay into bricks. Chopped straw was put with the clay to bind it, and then the sun would bake the clay hard so that when it was shaken from the moulds it had become brick.

Harder and harder grew the work, and more and more cruel grew the Egyptians, beating the slaves and forcing them to work until they dropped to the ground. And yet the Hebrews, the men of Israel, became even greater in numbers and spread still further over the land.

And then Pharaoh, seeing that no matter what he did the Hebrews were still greater in number, issued a stern decree.

'All the boy babies that are born must be taken from their mothers and thrown into the river Nile,' he commanded. 'Only the daughters may live.'

And then there was great weeping and wailing among the mothers who had baby sons, for all feared for their little ones.

Now there was a woman called Jochabed, who had a beautiful little son. She already had a daughter called Miriam, and another son, called Aaron. When her second little son was born to her, she looked at him and loved him. She could not bear to think that he should be thrown into the river. She made up her mind to hide him, so that no one should know of him.

So for three months she hid the child carefully, and the Egyptians did not know of him. He grew into a lovely baby boy, and when he was three months old his mother knew she could hide him no longer.

The baby had a lusty cry, and his mother was always afraid one of Pharaoh's soldiers would hear him. She could not bear the thought that he might be thrown into the river, where the crocodiles were. So she called her fifteen-year-old daughter Miriam and told her of her plan.

'I will make a little ark of bulrushes,' she said. 'I will make it quite water-tight, and we will line it softly. Then we will hide our baby in the reeds, near the pool where the Egyptian princess comes to bathe each day.'

Miriam ran to get the rushes out of which they could weave a little boat for the baby. Sometimes the peasant women crossed the river Nile, swimming strongly, and if they had a little baby to take with them they put him in one of these woven bullrush-boats, and pushed him in front of them all the way. So Miriam and her mother knew well how to make one.

They plaited a strong little ark for the baby, just the right size for him. They made a lid on a hinge, also out of bulrushes, so that he might be sheltered from the sun.

Then, just as Noah had done to his great wooden ark hundreds of years before, they daubed the strange little boat with slime and pitch, so that every crack and crevice was stopped and no water could get through. They set the little ark in the sun till it was quite dry.

'Now we will line it with soft blankets,' said Jochabed. So they put their best little rugs inside, and then placed the baby there. He looked so sweet that his mother could not keep from crying. He smiled up at her, a rosy, bonny child, and then closed his eyes in sleep.

'We will take him down to the river now and hide

Jochabed opened the lid to take a last look at the baby

him in the reeds,' said Jochabed. So, carrying the precious bulrush-boat between them, they slipped down to the river, crossing the fields when no one was about. Jochabed put the ark in some reeds near the pool where the daughter of Pharaoh came to bathe.

It floated beautifully. Jochabed opened the lid to take a last look at the sleeping baby, and then she closed it.

'Miriam, stay near and watch what happens to our baby,' she said, and went home with tears streaming down her face.

Miriam stayed nearby. She could see the boat from where she was. She listened for the baby to wake and cry, but he did not.

Now, at her usual time, the princess of Egypt came down to the river to bathe in her pool there, with her servant maids. She sent some of them to walk by the water, and she herself undressed with the help of her hand-maid.

As she was undressing she caught sight of something queer in the reeds by the bank. It looked like a little woven boat. What could it be?

The princess turned to her maid. 'Go and fetch that bulrush basket,' she said. 'It is strange that it should be there. I wonder what is inside it.'

Her maiden ran down to the reeds and picked up the plaited boat. It was heavy. She carried it back to her mistress and set it down before her.

Pharaoh's daughter lifted up the lid of the little boat. The baby inside awoke in fright and cried pitifully.

The princess gazed down at the lovely child and was full of pity and love for him. She took him from the basket and held him to her breast, trying to soothe him. She looked down at his small curly head, and he looked up at her out of serious dark eyes. Then he stopped crying and smiled suddenly up at her.

'This is one of the Hebrews' children,' said the princess, who knew that all baby boys were thrown into the river if they belonged to the slaves. 'How beautiful he is! How I wish he were my own son!'

She rocked him to and fro in her arms, looking down at the bonny child with delight. She was a kind and generous girl, and she longed to save the baby from being thrown into the river.

Now Miriam, his sister, had been watching all this in excitement. She had seen the maid picking up the basket. She had seen the princess opening the lid, and she had heard the baby crying. To her joy she saw that the beautiful princess loved the baby, so she was not afraid to go up and speak to her.

The girl went near to Pharaoh's daughter and bowed low. 'Shall I go and fetch a nurse for you from the Hebrew women, that she may nurse the child?' she asked, her dark eyes shining anxiously.

The princess looked at the young girl and smiled. 'Go,' she said. And Miriam sped away joyfully to find her mother.

Jochabed was waiting anxiously for news of the baby. Miriam's face told her the good news as soon as she saw her.

'Mother! The princess came and found our baby! She loved him, and she told me to fetch someone to nurse him!' cried the girl joyfully. 'Come, mother – our baby is safe. Come quickly.'

Jochabed hurried down to the river. As soon as she

reached the little group there, her eyes looked for her baby son. He was safe in the princess's arms!

Pharaoh's daughter looked up and saw Jochabed. She held out the baby to her. At once the child smiled and reached out his chubby arms. And then the princess guessed that Jochabed was his own mother.

'Take this child away,' she said to Jochabed. 'Nurse him for me, and I will give you wages to be his nurse. He shall be my son when he is old enough.'

Jochabed took her baby, with joy and thankfulness in her heart. The day would come when he must leave her and go to the palace, to be brought up as an Egyptian prince – but that day seemed far off, and the only thing that mattered now was that Jochabed had her baby safe in her arms again, and need not be troubled in case the soldiers found him. She need hide him no longer, for Pharaoh's daughter would give orders that he was to be nursed until he was old enough to be brought to her.

The princess bathed and then went back to the palace thinking of the day when the lovely baby would be old enough to be hers. She made many plans for him. He should have his own servants, he should be taught many things, he would grow up into a wonderful youth!

Jochabed and Miriam hurried home, with the tiny boy. They wept for joy as he was fed, and told their friends of their great good fortune. Now he need not be hidden away!

For some time he lived with his mother and father, his sister Miriam, and his brother Aaron. Then, when he was old enough to leave his mother, she took him to the palace.

The princess marvelled to see what a beautiful child he had become. She looked on him with love and pride.

'He shall be as my own son,' she said, 'and I will call him "Moses", which means "Drawn out of the water".'

11
The Burning Bush

Moses was brought up as a little Egyptian prince. He learnt all the Egyptian ways and customs, and he fought in Pharaoh's army. He was a wise youth, quiet and thoughtful, but with a temper that sometimes led him to do fierce things.

He was clever and a born leader. The princess was proud of him, but as he grew into manhood Pharaoh disliked him, fearing that he might one day join the enemies of the Egyptians and use his knowledge against them.

Moses knew that he was born of a Hebrew family. He knew that the slaves he saw in the land were his own race, and that although he had been brought up as an Egyptian prince, he really belonged to the Hebrew race. His mother had told him this many years before.

Moses hated to see the Hebrew slaves toiling in the hot sun at such hard tasks. He could not bear to see them tormented and beaten. He watched sometimes when he was in the brick fields, and saw that even when the slaves had worked their utmost, and were almost falling to the ground with weariness, the taskmasters lashed them with whips and would give them no rest.

One evening, when he was returning to the palace, he saw an Egyptian beating a young Hebrew. He lashed him so cruelly, and the youth cried out so piteously that Moses could not bear the sight. Anger flamed suddenly in him and he ran up to the Egyptian. He struck him and killed him.

Then, in fear and sorrow, he buried the man in the sand and fled back to the palace, hoping that no one had seen or heard.

Next day he went to the brickfields and saw two of the Hebrews fighting one another. He went to separate them and reproached them.

'Why must you strike one another? Surely you should help one another?'

One of the men answered roughly: 'Who made you a prince and judge over us? Are you going to kill me as you killed the Egyptian yesterday?'

Moses heard these words in horror. So it was known that he had struck and killed the Egyptian the day before. He knew that if it came to Pharaoh's ears he himself would be killed.

There was nothing else to do but go away. So Moses left the palace and fled away to the land of Midian, where he knew he would be safe. He left behind him all the riches and power that had been his. He was no longer an Egyptian prince, but a Hebrew shepherd, for he helped to guard the flocks of Jethro, the father of his wife.

In the land of Egypt the Hebrew slaves still groaned and wept under their cruel taskmasters. They cried out to God, praying him to deliver them, and to take them to a land far away, the beautiful land of Canaan. God had once promised that this land should be their own.

God heard the cries of the slaves. He remembered

his promise. Where would he find a leader to take the Hebrews from Egypt into the land of Canaan?

There was only one man wise enough and strong enough to lead a great company of slaves away from Egypt. And that man was Moses. He had fought in Pharaoh's armies. He had had authority over others. He had never been a slave, but was a born leader. So God chose Moses as his leader.

He went to speak with Moses and to tell him that he had chosen him to deliver the Hebrews from Pharaoh.

Moses was with the flocks on a hillside. He sat there, lost in thought. Suddenly he saw a very strange sight.

Not far off there was a bush. As Moses gazed on it he saw that the bush was burning. A clear bright flame of fire burned throughout the bush, and yet the bush itself was not harmed. Not a leaf, not a blossom was scorched or withered. And yet the flame burnt high, and the bush was on fire.

Moses watched in wonder and awe. He could not believe that the bush was on fire and yet was not burnt.

'I will go and see this great sight,' said Moses in amazement. 'I will see why this bush is not burnt.'

So he rose and went near the burning bush. And the voice of the Lord God came out of the midst of the bush, loud and clear in the mountain air.

'Moses!' said the voice. 'Moses!'

And Moses answered in wonder, 'Here am I.'

Then the voice spoke again. 'Come no nearer. Take off your shoes, for the place whereon you stand is holy ground. I am your God and the God of your fathers.'

As Moses gazed on it he saw that the bush was burning

Then Moses hid his face, for he was afraid to look upon God. The voice spoke again.

'I have heard the groans and cries of my people in Egypt; I have heard them wailing under the lash of their taskmasters. I know their sorrows, and I am come down to save them. I will send you to Pharaoh, so that you may bring my people out of Egypt. You shall take them to a good land, a land flowing with milk and honey.'

But Moses was afraid. 'Who am I, Lord, that I should go to Pharaoh? He would not let me bring the slaves out of Egypt. Neither will the Hebrews themselves listen to me for they will not believe that I have been with you this day.'

Then the voice came again. 'What is that you have in your hand?'

And Moses answered in surprise, 'My staff.'

And the voice said, 'Cast it on the ground.' Moses obeyed, and lo, it became a snake, and Moses fled away in fright. But the Lord said, 'Put out your hand and take it by the tail.'

In fear Moses obeyed. And as soon as he touched the snake it became his staff again, the same that he used for his sheep.

Then Moses knew that God would indeed help him in his great task, and would give him power to bring the Hebrew people out of Egypt into the Promised Land. God told him also to take Aaron his brother with him to help him. He was to take his staff too, so that he might show Pharaoh wonders with it.

Although he was fearful, and amazed that God should have chosen him for his leader, Moses at last promised to go to Pharaoh and tell him that he must set God's own people free.

Then the flame in the burning bush died. The voice came no more. God had gone from the bush, and from the quiet mountain-side.

12
Moses Rescues the Hebrew Slaves

Moses could not forget the strange burning bush and the voice of God. He knew that he must go to Egypt and do as God had said, but he remembered how he had once killed a man there, and he was afraid.

Then the voice of God came to him again. 'Go, return to Egypt. The men that would punish you are dead.'

So Moses took his wife and sons and went back to Egypt. In his hand was his staff, which God had once so strangely turned into a snake. On the way he met his brother Aaron, and told him all that had happened.

'I will go with you,' said Aaron. 'You shall tell me all that we must say, for I have the gift of words and you have not.'

So they went down into Egypt, and when they were there they gathered together the chief men of the Hebrews and told them what God had said on the mountain-side, from the burning bush. Then all the people were glad, for they hoped that their days of sorrow were soon coming to an end.

Moses and Aaron went to see Pharaoh. The king, who was not the same Pharaoh in whose palace Moses had been brought up, was told that there were two rough shepherds who wanted to speak with him.

'Why do you wish to speak with me?' demanded Pharaoh.

'Thus says the Lord God,' answered Moses. 'Let

the Hebrew people go, for the Lord wishes them to make a feast with him in the wilderness.'

Pharaoh laughed scornfully. 'Who is this Lord God that I, Pharaoh, should obey him? I know not the Lord, neither will I let the slaves go.'

Then Pharaoh gave orders that the taskmasters should be even harder to the slaves. 'You shall not even give them the straw to mix with their bricks,' he said. 'They must find their own straw – but yet they must still make the same number of bricks for me.'

And then the poor slaves were in a worse plight than before, for now they had to go out to gather straw and yet they still had to make the same number of bricks. They cried out in sorrow to Moses and Aaron.

Once again the two brothers went to see Pharaoh. The king scorned them, and Moses knew it was time to give Pharaoh a sign that God's power was behind him.

He threw his staff on the ground before the king and his men. When it touched the ground, it became a snake, just as it had done upon the mountainside.

But Pharaoh looked on the miracle with scorn. He called for his own magicians and wise men, and commanded that they should use the magic they knew to make their own staffs change into serpents.

And so powerful was the magic of the Pharaoh's magicians that they too changed their staffs into serpents. But, to the surprise of all those watching, Moses' snake swallowed all the others.

Still Pharaoh would not believe that Moses had been sent by God to plead for his people. He would not believe that it was God's own power that did signs and wonders by the hand of Moses. He refused to let the Hebrews go, and they groaned under the cruelty of the Egyptians.

Then God did many more wonders through his servant Moses, but still Pharaoh would not let the people go. He became frightened, but he was obstinate and angry.

But at last he had to let them go, because he saw that there was nothing else to do. God prepared a terrible punishment for him, so that even Pharaoh himself had to give way.

'I will slay the first-born in every house in Egypt,' said God. 'But the first-born of my own people I will not touch. Mark the doors of your houses with blood so that I may know my own people. Eat your last meal in haste tonight, with your shoes on your feet, and your staff in your hands. I will pass through the land of Egypt this night, to punish Pharaoh and his people, but your houses will I pass over, and your first-born shall not die. This feast, the last that you shall eat in the land of Egypt, shall be known as the Feast of the Pass-Over, and you shall tell it to your children, and to your children's children, so that it may never be forgotten.'

Then Moses and Aaron told all the Hebrews what God had said, and they prepared their last feast in Egypt that night. They marked their doors with blood, even as God had said, and they ate their meal in haste, with their shoes on their feet and their staff in their hand.

Then God passed through the land, and punished Pharaoh and his people as he had said. There arose a great weeping and wailing when it was found that the first-born in each house was dead. And so great was the sorrow that Pharaoh, whose first-born son was also dead, knew that he dared no longer keep the Hebrews in his land. Moses and Aaron must take them away before more evil came to Egypt.

Then Pharaoh sent to Moses and Aaron in the middle of the night. 'Rise up,' he commanded. 'Go forth out of Egypt at once, you and all your people. Go and serve your God. Take your flocks and your herds and be gone.'

Then in great gladness of heart the Hebrews rose up and prepared to go. They put their goods on their asses, they carried loads on their shoulders, they awoke their children and led them out of their houses.

The Egyptians pressed round them, urging them to go quickly. They were now afraid of these slaves that they had tormented so cruelly. They put gold into their hands, they gave them rings and jewels, they begged them to leave at once.

'We shall all die soon, if these people do not go!' they said to one another.

And so, laden with much gold and jewels, the Hebrews left the land of Egypt, led by Moses and Aaron, and set out on their long journey to the Promised Land.

13
A Strange Journey

The Hebrews never forgot that strange night when they left Egypt, urged on by the frightened Egyptians. They took their flocks and herds with them, and all their belongings, and it was indeed a great company that moved along the roads out of Egypt.

God would not let Moses take the people the shortest way, through the land of the Philistines, for they might have had to fight, and they were not prepared for battle. He told Moses to lead the people into the wild country that lay round about the Red Sea.

So that Moses might know the right way to go, God put a great pillar of cloud into the sky. This showed them the direction in which they had to travel.

By night, when a cloud would not be seen, God put a pillar of flame in the sky. All the people saw it and marvelled. They could not lose their way when God guided them so surely.

They went slowly, for their flocks and herds could not walk quickly. They were glad to have left behind their hard days of slavery, and they sang as they went.

But back in Egypt Pharaoh was full of anger. He had lost thousands of slaves who worked for nothing. Now his Egyptians must do the work instead. He had lost his first-born son whom he loved. He thought of Moses, and he hated him with a deep and bitter hatred. He hated all the Hebrews. He wished he had them in his power, so that he might punish them, and kill them.

Instead, what had happened? They had gone from Egypt with all their flocks and herds, their possessions – and had also taken with them much of the gold and rich jewels of his own people. Pharaoh brooded over this, and was sorry that he had let the slaves go.

His spies came in to see him. They had followed the Hebrews to see where they would go. They had even mixed with them in their camps, listening to their plans. Now they had come to report to their master.

'The Hebrews go, but they go slowly,' said the spies. 'They are guided by a pillar of cloud in the sky by day, and a pillar of fire by night. They are encamped on the shores of the Red Sea.'

Pharaoh listened, and his heart became hard with hate.

'We could trap them there,' he said, and he smiled cruelly. 'We will pursue them. We will send after them my swiftest chariots, and behind shall come my army. We will fall upon the Hebrews and slay them every one.'

Now the Hebrews were camping in peace by the shores of the Red Sea. They had set watchers around the camp for fear of enemies, and these men suddenly saw a cloud of dust in the distance.

They called to one another and pointed it out. What could it be? It was so big that it must be made by many people.

The dust-cloud was made by the advancing chariots of Pharaoh's army. He had taken six hundred chariots, with swift horses, and had bade them pursue after the escaping Hebrews. Behind them would come other chariots, and the whole of Pharaoh's army. But it was the first six hundred chariots that had raised the cloud of dust.

The camp-watchers gazed at the cloud in fear. And then they heard the thunder of hooves and wheels. The noise reached the camp, and everyone heard it. It was a curious, rumbling, thudding sound, and the Hebrews stopped their tasks in fear and dismay.

'The Egyptians have come after us!' they cried. 'Now what are we to do? There is no way of escape for us, for the wilderness is beyond us, and the sea bars our way!'

Mothers clasped their young children to them, and the men ran to get what arms they had. They had been slaves for so long that they had forgotten how to fight. Even if they had known which way to go to escape, they were hemmed in with their flocks and herds.

Some of the men went to Moses and reproached him bitterly.

'It would have been better for us to have stayed in Egypt as slaves than to die out here in the wilderness!'

Moses knew better than anyone the terrible danger that the whole camp was in. He knew that no mercy could be expected from Pharaoh and his men. Now was the time that Moses could show he was a born leader.

'Fear not,' he said. 'Stand fast, and the Lord God will save you. You shall see the Egyptians no more after today. The Lord shall fight for you.'

Then Moses went down to the sea by himself and

cried out to his God. And God answered him comfortingly.

'Speak to the people and tell them that they may go on their way. Lift up your staff and stretch out your hand over the sea, and divide the waters. The people shall go through the midst of the sea on dry ground. I will make the Egyptians know that I am the Lord God.'

Moses stretched out his hand over the splashing waves that ran on to the sand, and he lifted up his staff. A strong wind began to blow from the east, bellowing over the sandy shore and around the camp. Huge waves began to rise on the Red Sea.

Then another strange thing happened. The pillar of cloud, which had stood before the people each day, now moved behind the camp, and hung in the sky between the Hebrews and the Egyptians. When night came it changed as usual to a glowing pillar of flame, and the Egyptians marvelled to see it. They were afraid to attack the Hebrews then, and waited for the dawn to come.

Now all that night the strong east wind blew with a mournful voice. It kept the children awake in the camp. It made the sheep and the cattle restless. It chilled the men watching over the camp. The Egyptians heard it too, and drew their cloaks around them.

The tide went out fast. The wind blew back the waves as it followed the tide. It blew back the waters so strongly that the bed of the sea showed like dry land. The wind had piled the waters up in such a way that it had made a pathway through the sea.

In the morning when daylight came, the Hebrews looked in amazement and fear at the sea. Before them was a great pathway through the sea, wide and dry. On either side of it were the waters, piled up by the strong wind like walls. It was strange to see.

'Now the Lord has saved us!' said Moses, in great joy and thankfulness. 'Come, my people. We will walk through the waters before the Egyptian camp awakes. Take your flocks and herds and follow me. This is the way that the Lord has prepared for us. Be not afraid but come.'

The Hebrews took their children and their goods, and made their way fearfully down to the edge of the shore. Where waves had lapped the night before there was now dry sand. Far away, heaped on either side, was the sea. The strong wind still blew, and mothers wrapped blankets around their young ones for it was cold.

Leading their sheep and their cattle the people walked on to the pathway that ran straight between the waters to the other side. They made no sound as they went, for they did not want their enemies to know what had happened. If only they could escape in safety down the strange way that God had made for them!

The way was not easy, for there were big and little rocks, and pools and quicksands to avoid. The bed of the sea smelt strongly too, for it was used to being covered, and now strange weeds and plants lay drying in the sun.

But steadily the people crossed the divided waters, and at last came safely to the other side. And the pillar of cloud, which had stood between them and the camp of the Egyptians, moved itself and now stood in front of them once more, showing them the way to go in the wilderness on the other side of the sea.

The Egyptians stirred themselves in their camp. They sent out scouts to see what the Hebrews were doing. Soon these men returned to the camp, looking white and frightened.

They had a strange tale to tell. 'The Hebrews are gone!' they said. 'They and their flocks and herds are all gone from the camp.'

'Where have they gone?' cried the captains, springing up in dismay.

'Sir, they have gone through the waters of the sea,' said the scouts. 'The sea is divided, and a broad path lies through it. Dry land has appeared in the midst of the sea, and on this the Hebrews are journeying across to the other side. They have escaped us.'

The captains knew well that Pharaoh would blame them bitterly if the slaves escaped. 'Sound the trumpets!' they ordered at once. 'Let every man go to his chariot.'

The trumpets sounded, and the drivers of the chariots and their bowmen leapt to get their horses and drive off. The air was filled with the thudding of hooves and the rumbling of wheels.

The drivers lashed their horses without mercy as they drove them swiftly to the camp where the Hebrews had spent the night. By now the great east wind had dropped, and clouds were filling the sky. It seemed as if a storm was coming.

The Egyptians saw the strange pathway of dry land stretching through the divided waters. They had no time to be afraid. They drove their chariots straight down the sandy shore, and on to the path that God had made for the Hebrews.

It was easy to see which way the slaves had gone, for so many thousands of men, women and animals could not pass without leaving many signs of their going. The Egyptians, lashing their horses in fury, drove over the sandy path that lay wide-stretched between the towering walls of water.

But now the water was beginning to seep back beneath the sands. They were soft and the wheels of the chariots sank deep. It was impossible for the chariots to keep in line. Some were so deeply sunk in the sand that they could not be moved.

The wheels fell away, and the frightened horses plunged and reared. The Egyptians shouted to one another and there was a great confusion. They drove more and more slowly, and soon there were scores of chariots whose sunk or broken wheels prevented them from going either forward or backward.

In a short while the Egyptians in front knew that it was impossible to go any further. They tried to drive back, or they leapt from their bogged chariots and tried to force their way through the oncoming army. There was even greater confusion, and the Egyptians began to be frightened.

Then Moses once more stretched out his hand over the sea. The Egyptians heard a terrifying roar as the waters rolled over the oozing sand towards them. They gave loud cries of despair, and struggled to flee from the oncoming waves. The waters met, and a great wave reared its head over the place where the strange pathway had stretched. There was no path now – only heaving restless sea over the heads of the vanished Egyptians.

Then indeed did the Hebrews know that God had saved them from the Egyptians. In awe and wonder they watched the waters of the sea return to their place and hide the enemy from their sight.

They sang a great song to the Lord as they journeyed on their way, for their hearts were very glad.

14
Signs and Wonders

The distance to the fair land of Canaan was not really very far, and even although the people had to go slowly because of their little children, and their flocks and herds, they need not have taken very long to arrive in safety in the Promised Land.

But they were a very long time on their journey, for they went through the wilderness, where God had to teach them many hard lessons. They grumbled easily against Moses, their leader, and even against God, who had shown them so many wonders.

Moses did many wonders on the great journey. Once, when the people were hungry and could find no food, they grumbled bitterly to Moses.

'Why did you not leave us in Egypt, where at least we had bread and meat? Are we all to die of hunger in this place?'

Then God spoke to Moses. 'Behold, I will rain bread from heaven for you.'

And it came to pass that in the morning the dew fell round about. The people were used to this and they took no notice. But when the sun came up and dried the dew something was left behind on the ground.

The children saw it and looked in wonder. It was like hoar-frost. 'What is this that is covering the ground?' said the children. 'It is small and round and white.'

'It is manna, a gift from heaven,' said the people, rejoicing.

'This is the bread which the Lord God has given you to eat,' said Moses. 'Gather it before the sun grows hot or it will melt. Let every man take what he can eat.'

So the people gathered up the manna, and ate it. They liked it because it tasted like wafers made with honey.

Then there came another day when the people journeyed to a place in the wilderness where there was no water to drink. They were thirsty and once again they grumbled bitterly to Moses.

'Have you brought us up out of Egypt so that we and our children shall die of thirst? Give us water that we may drink.'

And Moses prayed to God and said, 'What shall I do with these people? They are almost ready to stone me.'

And the Lord answered Moses: 'Go before the people to the big rock that is in Horeb, and take with you your staff. Strike the rock with it, and I will cause water to come out so that the people may drink.'

Then Moses obeyed and he went to the rock in Horeb. He struck it with his staff, and behold, water poured out of it, and the people drank and were no longer thirsty.

One day, when the people had been journeying for some months, they came to where great mountains towered up. One of the biggest was Mount Sinai, where clouds rolled and thunderous noises echoed around.

It was here that God said he wished to speak with

He struck it with his staff, and behold, water poured out of it

Moses. A trumpeting noise came down from the mountain and the people trembled, for they knew that God was near, on the great mountain above them.

'See, Moses goes up the mountain to meet with his God in the mists,' the people whispered to one another.

Moses disappeared, and was gone from them for many hours. When he came back he carried with him two big flat pieces of stone, on which were graven ten commandments that God had given to Moses for his people. Moses read these to the wondering people, and they knew they must try to keep them.

Yet another time Moses went up the mountain to speak with God, and this time God told him that the people were to make a wonderful tent for him, in which he might come near to his chosen ones.

And this was done. The people brought to Moses their gold and silver and jewels so that their holy tent, their first church, should be made wonderful and beautiful. They carried it with them wherever they went, and knew that always God was near to them as they journeyed on towards the Promised Land.

At last they reached the fair land of Canaan, and there they settled in peace, forty long years after Moses had led them out of Egypt.

15
The Story of Gideon

There came a time when enemies once more fell upon the Hebrews, or, as they were called, the Israelites.

The Israelites had settled in a fair land and tilled the ground, and kept flocks and herds. They grew grapes for wine and corn for food. They were happy and contented.

But, alas, when they saw that the men of that country prayed to idols, made of wood, and called these idols their gods, then the men of Israel did the same. They forgot their own God, who had brought them out from Egypt in safety, and they went to pray to the wooden images on the hillside.

Therefore it seemed like a punishment for them when enemies came upon them and took their harvest, leaving nothing for the Israelites at all.

The Israelites were taken by surprise the first time. Their harvests were good, and they were about to reap their fields and to make their wine.

Then one day there came a cry from a man on the hillside.

'A great crowd comes! See, there are camels by the thousand!'

Then the Israelites looked, and they saw that the newcomers were Midianites – they came led by their chiefs, men dressed like princes. Their bright cloaks flowed out in the wind as they rode proudly on their camels.

'Why have they come?' wondered the Israelites, and looked fearfully at their fair fields of waving corn.

The Midianites had come to take the harvests. They set up their black tents, and there were so many that the Israelites could not count them.

They robbed the Israelites of their food, and when the men came to fight for what they had grown for their families and flocks, the Midianites were so strong that they chased all the Israelites up into the hills.

Whilst their enemy was encamped on the plains, the Israelites did not dare to live there. They had to make themselves caves and dens in the hillside.

Sometimes the Midianites furled their black tents and left the land. Then the Israelites would rejoice and would go down from the hills to sow seed once again. But at harvest time their enemies would once more appear, and then the Israelites would lose the golden corn from their fields, the purple grapes from their vines, and they would be robbed of sheep and cattle, and even of any corn or wine they had already stored away.

They did not know what to do. There were so many Midianites that it was impossible to fight them. Soon the men of Israel were half starved, for what they sowed they were not allowed to reap.

Then they were sad, and they wondered how they would defeat such a mighty host as their enemy. There seemed no man who could lead them against the Midianites.

Now one day a young man called Gideon was at work secretly threshing corn in a big wine trough which was cut out of rock in the hillside. He threshed his corn there so that the enemy should not see him.

As he threshed he heard a voice speaking to him. 'The Lord is with you, mighty man of valour!'

Gideon looked from the wine trough in which he stood, and saw a stranger sitting under a nearby oak tree.

'Oh, sir,' he said, 'if the Lord is with us, why are we fallen under the hand of the enemy?'

'Behold!' said the stranger, 'you shall save your people from the Midianites.'

Gideon was amazed and doubtful. 'How can I do that?' he asked. 'My family is poor and I am the least in my father's house.'

'I will be with you,' said the stranger, and then Gideon knew that he must be talking with God or with his angel.

He was afraid, and could hardly believe that this was so. He longed for a sign so that he might know for certain that he had been chosen by God to save his people.

'Do not go yet,' said Gideon. 'I will give you meat and bread and broth.' So he went to fetch these things and presently brought them out.

Then the angel of God spoke again to him. 'Lay the food upon the rock and pour out the broth.'

So Gideon did so, and the angel put out his staff and touched the things that the young man had brought. In an instant fire came up out of the rock and swallowed everything upon it. Then the angel vanished and Gideon was alone.

Gideon thought a great deal about the angel and what he had said. He saw the wooden images of Baal on the hillside, and he was ashamed because the Israelites prayed to them instead of to the true God.

He made up his mind that he would throw them down that night, and would build a stone altar for his own God, the God who had brought his people safely out of Egypt.

So that night he took ten servants and went to the hillside. He did not dare to do such a thing in the daytime, for he was afraid that the people would stop him. He and his servants threw down the wooden images there, and then built a new altar of stones. They prayed to their own God, and then crept secretly home.

In the morning the men passing by were astonished and horrified to see the idols thrown down. They ran to see what had happened and talked to one another. 'Who has done this thing? Who has cast down the images of Baal, our god?'

Then someone gave the secret away. 'It is the young man Gideon, the son of Joash, who has done this.'

Then the men went to the house of Joash and they called to him: 'Bring out your son Gideon, for he must die. He has dared to throw down the images of Baal.'

And Joash answered loudly: 'Let Baal come himself to fetch Gideon! If he is indeed a powerful god, as you say, let him then come in anger and plead for himself!'

But Baal did not come, for he was only a wooden idol, and so Gideon was not put to death. He told the story of the angel to all who would listen, and soon people began to say that the young man Gideon had been sent to be their leader.

Now at the next harvest-time not only the Midianites came to steal the corn and the wine from the men of Israel, but also many of their friends. Gideon watched the black tents being put up in the valley below, and he saw that there were so many that surely there would be nothing left for the Israelites when the enemy had taken what they would.

Then Gideon blew a trumpet, and he sent messengers throughout the land, bidding the young men come to him to fight against the enemy. But when he had sent his messengers Gideon felt doubtful about his own powers. Did God really mean that he would help him to save his people?

Gideon spread a fleece of wool on the ground. 'Now,' he said, 'if God, who sends the dew each night, will send it only on my fleece, and not on the ground around, then I shall surely know that I am to save my people.'

The next morning Gideon arose very early. He was anxious to see what had happened to his fleece. To his joy it was soaked with the dew – but all the ground nearby was dry. Gideon picked up the fleece, and it was heavy with the dew. He wrung it out, and from it he filled a bowl full of water.

The next night God caused the fleece to be dry, but the ground to be wet. And then Gideon felt sure of himself and knew that God had chosen him out to save his people.

Soon so many came to fight under Gideon's leadership that he had a great army.

'We shall be able to defeat the Midianites,' said the young men proudly. 'There are twenty-two thousand of us. Of our strength and might shall we be able to conquer the enemy.'

But God did not want the young men to become vain and proud. So he spoke to Gideon and said: 'There are too many of your people gathered here. Go to them and say that all those who are afraid may return home.'

So Gideon gave God's message, and so many returned home that there were only ten thousand left.

But even so, that was a big army. God spoke again to Gideon. 'There are still too many. Take them down to the water, and I will tell you which of them to choose to stay and fight, and which to go home.'

So Gideon took the men down to the water, and they knelt there to drink. He watched them as they drank. Some went down on their knees and drank from the river itself. Others took water into their hands and lapped it.

'Put aside those that lap the water from their hands,' said God. 'Those are the men I choose. The rest must return home. With these three hundred men will I save you and your people from the Midianites.'

So Gideon sent away every man except the three hundred that had taken up water in their hands. Then his army was indeed small, but it was enough.

That night Gideon looked down into the valley and saw the numbers of the enemy, and he was afraid. Their tents stretched for miles, and their camels were without number. How could he, a young man who had never fought before, take such an army with only three hundred men?

He crept down the hillside with his servant, Phurah. He came to a tent and heard the soldiers inside talking to one another. Gideon could hear clearly what they said.

'Behold!' said a soldier, 'I dreamed a dream, and this was my dream. A cake of barley tumbled right into the armies of the Midianites, and it came to a tent

99

and struck it, so that the tent fell to the ground. Now what can such a dream mean?'

And another answered at once: 'It means that Gideon, the son of Joash, will overturn the armies that go against him!'

Then Gideon's heart lifted for joy and he went back to his men, rejoicing. He spoke to them of the plan that God had put into his mind to overcome the enemy.

'Arise!' said Gideon, 'for this night you shall conquer the Midianites!'

Then he divided the three hundred men into three companies. To each man he gave some strange things – a trumpet, an empty pitcher or jar, and a torch.

'Place your torch inside your pitcher,' he commanded, 'so that the enemy shall not see its light until the time comes. The pitcher will hide the flame of the torch.'

So every man put his torch inside his jar, and the light was hidden there. Only the smoke came out, but it was night-time, and it could not be seen.

'You must do all that I do,' said Gideon to his men. 'I am going to take you down to the camp of the enemy. We shall surround it. Make no noise until you hear me sound my trumpet. Then you must blow your trumpets, too. And as you blow them you must shout out with a loud voice, "The sword of the Lord and of Gideon!"

'Your pitchers also you must break, so that suddenly, all around the camp, the Midianites will see torches flashing, and will hear trumpets blowing. Then they will think there is a great army surrounding them, and will think that each torch is the sign of a whole company of men, instead of only one man.'

The men listened in silence, holding their pitchers and their trumpets. Then they followed Gideon quietly down the hillside to where the countless tents of the Midianites lay spread out in the valley below. They surrounded the camp, and the enemy did not know they were there.

Suddenly Gideon blew his trumpet loudly and it rang out clearly through the night air. Almost at the same moment the rest of the men blew theirs, too, and the enemy awoke in alarm, and sprang to their feet, rushing outside their tents to see what was happening.

Then, in the darkness of the night, many brilliant torches suddenly flashed out as each of Gideon's men smashed his pitcher, and took his flaming torch to wave round his head. Loud voices shouted: 'The sword of the Lord and of Gideon! The sword of the Lord and of Gideon!'

The Midianites were terrified. They really thought that an enormous army was surrounding them, for there were lights all round the camp, trumpets blowing everywhere and voices shouting. Thinking that the enemy had come right into their camp, they rushed out into the night to find him.

They fell into each other as they went, and, taking their swords, they began to strike about wildly. They hit one another, and cried in pain and terror. Soon the whole of the enemy were in flight, thinking that the men of Israel were upon them. Gideon and his men chased them, shouting wildly.

When the people heard that Gideon had defeated

the enemy, they were glad. Word went round the whole countryside, and the name of Gideon was in every man's mouth.

'We will make him our king,' said the people. 'He has won a great victory over an enemy that has robbed us of our harvests for seven long years. Now the Midianites are fled, and we will make Gideon our ruler and our king.'

So they sent to him, and told him they would have him for their king. 'Rule over us,' they said. 'You shall be king, you, and your son, and your son's son, for you have saved us from a terrible enemy.'

But Gideon would not rule over them. 'I will not be your king,' he said. 'And neither shall my son rule over you. But the Lord God shall rule over you.'

16
The Giant Samson

There once lived a giant of a man called Samson, and he hated the Philistines, who were the enemies of the men of Israel.

From his boyhood Samson had been enormously strong, and all his enemies feared him. He was a tall, broad man, with long hair that fell around his shoulders, for he had never had it cut in his life.

One day, it is said, as he climbed the hillside, he heard a roaring, and suddenly he saw before him a young lion, strong and fierce, lashing his tail, and snarling at Samson.

The young man did not run away. He pounced forward on the lion, and tore him to pieces. Then he threw the dead lion into the bushes and went on his way.

When he came back that way some days later, he remembered the lion he had killed and he turned aside to look for it. He heard a humming of bees and looked to see where the noise came from. To his surprise he saw that the body of the dead lion had been picked to the bare bones by the crows, and that some wild bees had built their hive inside the body.

Samson took out the honeycomb and ate it. 'Out of the eater came forth meat, and out of the strong came forth sweetness,' said Samson, and laughed at his fancy.

Samson hated the Philistines, for this enemy had

conquered the men of Israel, and made them pay tribute to them. Sometimes the tribute was gold, sometimes it was goods. Samson used his great strength against the Philistines and played many tricks on them.

Once he went down to their city, and with his own hand slew thirty of the enemy. Some time later, when they had done something to grieve and anger him, he sat upon the hillside and brooded over his wrongs until he thought of a way to revenge himself.

There were wild foxes and jackals in the hillside. Samson began to hunt them out. One by one he caught them, not caring anything for their snarling and snapping. He caught at least three hundred and penned them up.

Then he made fire-brands, and when they were ready, he went to where he had penned up the foxes. He caught the foxes in pairs with his hands, and tied them together by the tail. Between the tails he tied a fire-brand. The frightened animals snapped and bit but Samson did not care.

Below, in the valley, were the corn-fields of the Philistines, golden and ripe, ready for harvesting. There were their vine-yards too, bursting with purple grapes, their olive-yards full of olive trees. Samson looked down on this fair sight, which would bring much corn, wine and oil to his enemy, and smiled grimly.

He lighted the fire-brand between the tails of the first pair of foxes. It flared up, and frightened the poor animals. Samson clapped them on the back, set them free, and they tore down the hill together, snapping and snarling in panic.

They could not get away from one another, for their tails held them together. The fire-brand burned down and scorched their hair. They ran right down the hillside and into the wide-spread corn-fields of the Philistines.

Samson was busy tying another pair of foxes together by the tail, a fire-brand between. This he lighted too and set the foxes free, rushing down the hill towards the corn-field.

The corn was dry and ripe. The fire-brands set light to the stalks, and the flames spread rapidly all over the field. More and more foxes tore into the fields and grape-vines, bringing fire and destruction.

Soon clouds of smoke arose from the fields and the Philistines rushed out in alarm. What was happening? Then they saw the foxes, racing through the corn, tied together, bringing fire with them. Dozens of them, scores of them, tearing along in fright and pain.

The fire spread. It reached the vine-yards and burnt those down. It went to the olive-yards, and soon the valuable olive-trees were blackened and burnt. The Philistines could not save anything.

'Who has done this?' they cried.

'Samson has done it,' was the answer.

The Philistines made up their minds that they would capture Samson and slay him. So they marched into the land where the Israelites lived, and pitched their tents there.

'Why have you come against us?' asked the men of Israel.

'We come for Samson,' answered the Philistines. 'We shall bind him and punish him for what he has done.'

Then three thousand of the men of Israel went to find the giant Samson. They found him on the hills and spoke to him.

'You know that the Philistines are our conquerors and rule over us. Why must you anger them? We are come now to bind you and deliver you up to the enemy, for we will not have our country over-run by them.'

Samson looked at his people for a while and then asked them a question. 'If I let you bind me and take me to the enemy, will you promise that you will not harm me yourselves?'

'We shall not kill you,' said the Israelites, 'but we shall surely deliver you to the Philistines.'

Then Samson let them bind him tightly with two new cords, and they led him down the hill to the Philistines.

As the Israelites came down the hill with Samson, the watching Philistines gave a shout of joy.

'The giant comes! Samson is bound! Now he is in our power!'

The men of Israel led Samson right up to the Philistines – but suddenly the giant snapped the two new ropes that bound him as if they had been cotton! He saw the old jaw-bone of an ass lying nearby and he picked it up. With this as a weapon he rushed in among the astonished enemy, and killed a thousand of them. They fled away before him and the Israelites shouted to see them go.

Samson sang loudly in triumph. 'With the jaw-bone of an ass, heaps upon heaps, with the jaw of an ass have I slain a thousand men.'

Then the Israelites made him their judge, for they

thought him a great and powerful man. Many marvellous deeds he did that are told of to this day.

One of them he did when he went to visit a city belonging to his enemy. He entered the gates, and when it was known that he was in the city, the men there hastened to shut and fasten the gates so that they might catch Samson when he departed.

But in the night Samson arose, and went to go out of the gates. He found they were locked, and in anger he took the gates and the pillars bodily out of the ground and carried them away with him. He carried them on his shoulder up to a hill in the distance, and there threw them away.

The Philistines hated and feared the giant Samson. Always they waited, hoping that one day they would capture him and punish him for what he had done to them. And at last it seemed as if their chance had come.

Samson loved a Philistine woman called Delilah. When the Philistine chiefs heard of this they went secretly to Delilah and spoke with her.

'Find out how it is that Samson is so strong, and find out if there is any way of robbing him of his strength,' they said. 'If you do this, and tell us, we will give you much silver.'

Delilah promised to find out. So the next time that Samson came to see her, she begged him to tell her if there was anything that would make him as weak as other men.

He laughed at her, and, because he liked a joke, he said, 'If I am bound with seven green withes that have never been dried, then I shall be as weak as other men.'

Delilah told the Philistines and they were glad. When next Samson visited Delilah some of the men hid themselves in readiness to spring upon Samson when he was bound.

Delilah had the seven green withes ready. They were supple, and she bound his hands easily, laughing as she did so. 'Now you are at my mercy!' she said. And Samson smiled also. Delilah waited until he was asleep, and then she called out loudly, as a sign to the waiting Philistines:

'Samson, Samson, the Philistines are upon you!'

Samson leapt up, and broke his bonds easily. He escaped out of the house, and left the Philistines behind. When next he came to her, Delilah grumbled at him.

'Behold, you mocked me and told me lies. Now tell me truly how you may be bound, so that you will be weak.'

And again Samson joked with her, telling her that if he were bound with new ropes that had never been used before, then he would not be able to set himself free.

So Delilah, as if in fun, bound him with new ropes, and, when he was asleep, called out loudly to warn the men who were lying in wait. 'Samson, the Philistines are upon you!'

And again Samson broke his bonds and fled away easily. Then Delilah again reproached him, and begged him to tell her the truth. And he laughed once more and said, 'Well, bind the seven plaits of my long hair into the web of your loom, and fasten it with a pin. Then I shall be unable to free myself.'

So Delilah took the seven braids of his long hair,

and wove it tightly into the web of her loom, which was fastened to the ground by wooden posts. She fastened it with her pin. Samson slept whilst she did this, and suddenly she awoke him, crying as she had done before, 'Samson, the Philistines are upon you!'

He awoke as the men came out of their hiding-place to capture him. He leapt to his feet, and with a great heave of his strong shoulders he pulled Delilah's loom out of the ground, posts and all, and fled away with them still swinging from his hair.

And now Delilah began to reproach him very bitterly indeed. 'How can you say you love me when you mock me and tell me lies? I do not believe you love me, or you would tell me what I ask.'

For many days Delilah spoke to Samson in this way, and he grew vexed. 'I will tell you wherein my great strength lies,' he said at last. 'It is simple to tell – as long as my hair is not shaven from my head, I am strong. If my hair were shaven away, then I should be weak.'

Then Delilah rejoiced, for this time she felt sure that Samson had told her the truth. The next time he was asleep, she sent for a man and bade him cut off the braids that Samson wore, and to shave his head. And the man did so.

Then Delilah called out loudly as before, 'Samson, the Philistines are upon you!'

And he awoke and tried to escape away as he had done before. But he could not for his strength was gone, and God was not with him.

So the Philistines caught him and they punished him for his wrong-doing to them, most cruelly and

The next time he was asleep she sent for a man and bade him cut off the braids that Samson wore

terribly, for they blinded him so that he could no longer see.

They bound him in chains and put him in the prison-house to grind corn. And there was Samson, all the day long, grinding corn for the Philistines, a blind and unhappy giant of a man.

But his hair once more began to grow, and he felt his strength returning to him.

Then one day the Philistines held a great feast, and they remembered Samson. 'Let us fetch him and make him show us his strength,' they said. 'We will make sport of him. He is blind now, and bound. He can do us no harm.'

So they sent for him and a boy led him to where they held their feast. They made him show them feats of strength, and laughed at him.

When they had finished with him, Samson spoke to the boy who led him. 'Take me to the pillars upon which this house is built,' he said. 'I would lean upon them and rest.'

So the boy took him to the great pillars of the house. On the flat roof of the house were about three thousand men and women who had been watching Samson, and below, in the house itself were many others. Then Samson called out to God, and begged him to remember him.

'Lord God, remember me, I pray, and give me my strength back only this once, so that I may be avenged of the Philistines for my two blind eyes.'

And Samson took hold of the two middle pillars upon which the house was built, and which held it up, one pillar in his right hand and the other in his left.

'Let me die with the Philistines!' said Samson, and he bowed himself with all his might, dragging at the two enormous pillars. They broke and the house fell down upon all the lords of the Philistines, and upon everyone there.

So died the giant Samson. Never has there been another man as strong as he.

17
Ruth the Gleaner

In the little town of Bethlehem, where Jesus was to be born many years later, there lived a woman called Naomi. She was happy with her husband and two young sons. She lived in one of the little white houses that clustered round about the hill of Bethlehem, and the people there knew her and liked her well, because she was sweet-tempered and pleasant.

But there came a day when famine came to Bethlehem. The harvests failed, and there was nothing to eat. Naomi's husband made up his mind to leave Bethlehem and to go to the land of Moab, where there was plenty to eat.

So Naomi left behind the town she knew and loved, and went with her husband and two little sons to Moab.

Then a great sorrow came to Naomi, for her husband died, and she was left alone with her two little sons. She worked for them and took care of them. They grew into young men, and they married. One married a Moabite maiden called Orpah, and the other a maiden called Ruth.

Naomi loved both her new daughters, and they loved her. She looked forward to seeing her grandsons – but alas for Naomi, before either of her two new daughters had any children, her two sons died. Then indeed was Naomi unhappy, for now she had lost her husband, her sons and could no longer look forward to seeing her sons' sons.

'I cannot stay in this land,' said Naomi to her daughters-in-law. 'I remember the lovely hill-town of Bethlehem, with its beautiful views, its little white houses, and its kindly folk. They are my own people and I shall return to them in my sadness.'

So she packed up her few belongings and made ready to go. Orpah and Ruth set off with her, but when they had gone a little way, Naomi spoke to them.

'Go, return to your mother's house,' she said. 'You have been very kind to me and to my two dead sons and may the Lord deal as kindly with you.'

Then she kissed them and said good-bye, weeping, for she loved them. Orpah and Ruth wept too, and they said, 'Surely we will go back with you to your people.'

And Naomi said, 'Turn again, my daughters. Why should you want to go with me? Turn again, my daughters, and go your way.'

Then Orpah turned back, and went the way they had come. But Ruth would not go.

'Behold!' said Naomi, 'your sister-in-law has gone back to her own people. Go after her, Ruth, and return too.'

But Ruth said: 'Ask me not to leave you, for where you go I will go, and where you stay I will stay. Your people shall be my people and your God shall be my God. Where you die I will die and there will I be buried. Nothing but death shall part us.'

Then Naomi saw that the young girl had made up her mind not to leave her, and she let her come with her. Her heart was glad to think she had such a loving friend, for she felt very lonely.

They journeyed on until at last they came to Bethlehem. The people saw them coming, and they came out to see who the strangers were. They did not know the lovely young girl, Ruth, who was dressed in the dress of a Moabite woman. But after a while they thought they knew Naomi.

Could it be Naomi? She had left Bethlehem as a happy young woman with her husband and two sons – and this looked to be an old, unhappy woman, her face lined with sorrow.

'Is this Naomi?' they asked in wonder. The name 'Naomi' meant 'Pleasant', and Naomi answered sadly.

'Do not call me Naomi! Call me instead Mara which means bitter. For the Lord God has dealt very bitterly towards me. I went out with my husband and my sons and I come back without them.'

The people found Naomi a little house where she and Ruth might live. Naomi soon told everyone how kind and gentle Ruth was, and how she would not stay behind when Naomi wanted to return to Bethlehem. The people saw that Ruth helped Naomi all she could, and they liked her and spoke well of her.

Now, when they returned to Bethlehem it was the beginning of the barley harvest. Ruth looked down at the golden fields of corn, and she wondered if she could go and work there to get a little food for herself and Naomi, for they were very poor.

'Let me now go to the field,' she said to Naomi. 'I will glean corn there for us.'

'Go, my daughter,' said Naomi. And Ruth went down to the field. In those days, when men cut the

Soon she was busy picking up the stray ears of barley

shining corn with their curved sickles and bound it themselves, they very often dropped heads of the barley. Anyone might pick these up and keep them for themselves. They were called gleaners, because they gleaned the corn that was dropped.

Ruth looked to see where she might glean, and she went to a part of the field that belonged to a farmer called Boaz. Soon she was busy picking up the stray ears of barley.

Now later on Boaz the farmer came out from Bethlehem to see how his reapers were doing. He said to them: 'The Lord be with you!' And they answered him in their usual way, 'The Lord bless you!'

Then the farmer saw the strange young girl gleaning with the others, and he wondered who she was.

'Who is this girl?' he asked, seeing that she was not dressed like the other women of the town.

His servant told him. 'It is the young girl who returned with Naomi from the land of Moab.'

And then Boaz was told all about Ruth – how kind and gentle she had been to her lonely mother-in-law, and how she was even now working for her. The servant told him how Ruth would not leave Naomi, and had come with her all the way from her own country.

Boaz looked at the young girl working so patiently in the hot sun, and he went over to her, wondering at her sweet face and patient eyes. He spoke gently to her.

'Hear what I say, my child. Keep here in this field by my maidens. No one shall hurt you. When you are thirsty you may go and drink water that has been set aside for the reapers.'

Ruth bowed herself down before him. 'Why are you so kind to me, a stranger?' she asked in wonder.

'I have heard of your great kindness to Naomi,' answered Boaz. 'God will reward you for your good deeds. At meal-times you must come to us in the shady part of the field and eat with us.'

So when the men and women stopped work in the fields and went to eat, Ruth went with them. Boaz was kind to her and gave her all she wanted to eat. When she got up to set to work again, Boaz spoke secretly to the reapers.

'Let her come close to you when she gleans and do not send her away. And drop some handfuls of corn on purpose for her, so that she may pick them up.'

So the reapers did so, and dropped many ears of corn for Ruth to glean. She had a great deal by the time the evening came. She beat out what she had gleaned and carried it home to Naomi.

Naomi was amazed to see all that Ruth had brought, for it was very much. Some could be put away for the winter, for there was more than enough for the day.

'Where did you glean?' asked Naomi. 'Someone must have been very good to you.'

'I worked in a field belonging to a man called Boaz,' said Ruth. 'He was very kind to me.'

'Now blessed be God,' said Naomi, 'for he shows kindness to me and my family. This man Boaz is a relation of yours, Ruth. Go out with his maidens, and do not go to any other field.'

So day after day Ruth went down to the fields of Boaz, and there she worked, and Boaz helped her all he could. When the barley harvest ended the wheat harvest began, and again Ruth worked steadily day by day.

Boaz watched her at work and heard everyone talking of the gentleness and kindness of the girl from the land of Moab. He knew that she would make him a good and loving wife, and he made up his mind to marry her.

And so it came about that Ruth had her reward, for she married the kind Boaz, and lived happily with him. Naomi, too, was very happy, for once again she had a son to look after her. Boaz was good to her, and later on she was joyful because his little son, Ruth's baby, sat on her knee.

The women of the village were glad for Naomi. 'He is the son of your daughter-in-law, who loves you, and who is better to you than seven sons!' they said.

And as Ruth nursed her baby boy in the evenings, sitting on the hillside, looking across the quiet valley, she was filled with gladness that she had returned with Naomi and had not turned back with Orpah. Her faithful love had been rewarded.

18
The Child Who Was Given to God

The Holy Tent of God was on the top of the little Hill of Shiloh, kept by the priests who taught the people the word of God. Every year the Israelites came to a great festival, and then the green valley was covered with their dark tents.

One year a man called Elkanah came to the festival. He brought with him his whole family. He had two wives, Penninah and Hannah, and Penninah had children, but Hannah had none.

Everyone was happy and joyful at the festival, and they ate and drank and were glad. Only Hannah was sad. She would not eat or drink, for Penninah had been very unkind to her.

Penninah had laughed at her because she had no children. Hannah saw Penninah's boys and girls running about, and she was sad because she had none to run with them. She began to cry.

She left the feast and went up the hill of Shiloh towards the Tent of God. She went inside, and there, sitting in his seat, she saw the High Priest of the temple. This was the old man Eli. He was dressed very grandly, and Hannah felt half afraid of him, for he was the Judge of all Israel.

Hannah had come to tell God her trouble. She wept bitterly and begged God to give her a little son of her own.

'Oh, Lord God,' said Hannah, 'if only you will let

me have a son, I will give him back to you all the days of his life! Only let me have a son!'

Eli, the old priest, saw Hannah weeping and was sorry for her. 'Go in peace,' he said, 'and may the Lord God grant you what you wish!'

Then Hannah was glad, and she went back to her husband rejoicing. She knew that now she would have a little son of her own, and she waited patiently for that day to come.

When the baby was born she was full of joy. She called him Samuel, and looked down at him lovingly, for he was a very beautiful child. Her husband was glad, too.

'I will not go to the festival with you this year,' said Hannah. 'I will wait until Samuel is old enough to take with me, for I promised the Lord God I would give the boy back to him all the days of his life. Therefore, when he is older, and can leave me, I must take him to the High Priest and give him to God, so that he may serve in the Holy Tent and become a priest when he is grown.'

Samuel grew quickly. He was a strong and beautiful child, and his mother loved him with all her heart. She was sad when the day came at last when she must take him to Shiloh to the priest. But she had made a promise to God, and she must keep it.

So when the child was able to look after himself she went with her husband to the yearly festival at Shiloh. Samuel was excited at going on such a journey. Hannah kept him close to her, for she knew that very soon now she must part from him. She took with her presents for old Eli, and she wondered if he would remember her.

Eli looked at the beautiful child who stood wonderingly by Hannah

Hannah took Samuel by the hand when they reached the Holy Tent, and they went inside. She saw Eli sitting there, and spoke humbly to him.

'Oh, my lord, I am the woman who once came here and stood near you, praying to God and weeping. I prayed for this child, and God answered my prayer and gave him to me. Now I come to keep my promise to the Lord God and to lend him my child for the rest of his days.'

Eli looked at the beautiful child who stood wonderingly by Hannah. He took him and blessed him. Then Hannah kissed him good-bye and went out of the Holy Tent, her eyes full of tears. It was hard to give up her only son when he was so little.

Eli showed the child to the other priests. Two of these were his own sons, and they were wicked. Eli should not have allowed them to be priests serving God's holy temple, but he was weak, and did not turn them out.

The priests dressed the little boy just as they themselves were dressed, in a white linen robe and an embroidered girdle. They taught him many things to do in the temple. He mixed the spices for the incense that was burnt on certain days. He poured oil into the temple lamps, and lighted the floating wicks. He learnt many things, and he learnt them well.

Once every year, when the great festival came, Samuel's mother visited him. She was happy when the time came, for then she could see how her little boy had grown, and if he was happy.

Each year Hannah made him a little coat and brought it to him. She made it beautifully of the finest lambs' wool, which she spun herself. Each year she made a little bigger coat, for she knew her boy would have grown.

Samuel looked for her and welcomed her. He told her all he had learnt, and how he could read and write and how he had been taught God's laws.

Hannah looked at the child-priest and was glad she had given him to God, for she saw clearly that he was a good and happy child, and she hoped that in days to come he might be able to help his people. And, indeed, it was time that someone helped them, for they were forgetting many of the commandments of God, and some of them were forgetting even God himself. Eli's sons were wickeder than ever, and still the old priest did not turn them out of the temple.

Because of their wickedness many people had stopped coming to worship at the holy temple. Some of them began to pray to the wooden idols of Baal again. Evil was in the land of the Israelites once more.

Samuel grew older, and God saw him in the temple and loved the little child. One night he called to him and Samuel heard.

The boy had gone to sleep in the temple, and a voice awoke him by calling his name. Samuel sat up at once, thinking that Eli wanted him. He got up and ran to where the old priest lay.

'Here I am,' he said. 'You called me.'

'I didn't call you,' said Eli. 'Lie down again.'

Samuel went to lie down but again he heard a voice, and the voice said, 'Samuel!'

He once more went to Eli. 'Here I am,' he said, 'for truly you called me!'

And Eli answered in surprise, 'I didn't call you. Lie down again.'

Then a third time the voice came to the boy. 'Samuel!' And a third time Samuel went to Eli and said, 'Here I am, for surely you did call me.'

And then Eli knew that it must have been God who had called Samuel. 'Go and lie down,' he said. 'If you hear the voice calling you again, answer and say, "Speak, Lord, for your servant hears".'

So Samuel, half afraid and greatly wondering, went back to his mattress and lay down. He did not go to sleep, but lay listening, and in the silence of the temple the voice came again, 'Samuel, Samuel!'

The boy answered at once, 'Speak, Lord, for your servant hears.'

And then God told Samuel that he would have to punish Eli and his sons because they had done great wrong. Samuel listened in awe, for this was the first time that God had ever spoken to him. He lay awake until the morning, thinking over what God had said, frightened of telling Eli the message God had brought.

In the morning he arose and opened the doors of the temple wide. Eli saw him and called to him.

'Here am I,' said Samuel.

'What did the Lord God say?' asked Eli. 'Do not hide it from me, for I must know.'

And so Samuel told Eli, and the old man listened in sorrow. He knew that he had been weak with his sons and should not have allowed them in the temple of God. 'It is the Lord,' said Eli. 'Let him do what seems good.'

19
Samuel Chooses a King

The boy-priest grew up. Eli's sons were still allowed to serve in the temple, and to cheat the people who came to worship and pray, for Eli was too weak even to heed the warning of God. The old man was still the High Priest, but now Samuel was the one whose words were known throughout the land.

'He is a true man of God,' said the people. 'Let us go to Shiloh to hear his words.'

The years went by, and a great disaster came to Shiloh. The Philistines were at war with the Israelites, and Eli's sons went to fight. They took into battle with them the wonderful gold ark of God, out of the holy temple, thinking that God would surely fight on their side if the men carried his beautiful golden ark with them.

But they lost the battle, and the golden ark of God was captured by the enemy. Eli's two sons were killed, and the news was taken to Eli.

He died as soon as he had heard the terrible news. Then the Philistines came and killed the people of Shiloh and burnt down the holy Tent of God, robbing it of anything they could take away.

Samuel was full of sorrow to see the holy temple burnt down, and to hear the cries of the people of Shiloh. He fled away, and wandered round the countryside, trying to make the people understand that God would be with them again if only they would worship and trust him. The people listened to Samuel, for he was a wise and good man, and his name was known to them all.

Samuel judged the people of Israel for many years, and he made his sons judges over the people, too. But his sons were not good and wise as he was, and the people did not like them.

One day the old men of Israel went to Samuel and spoke with him. 'Behold, you are old!' they said, 'and your sons are not wise as you are. We would have you choose a king to rule over us as all the other nations have.'

'If you have a king as other nations have, then he will do the same as other kings,' said Samuel. 'He will take your sons for soldiers; he will make servants of your daughters; he will take of your money and your goods. And this you will cry against bitterly.'

But the Israelites would not listen to Samuel's words. 'Nay, but we will have a king over us,' they said. 'Then we shall be like the other nations. Our king will judge us, and go before us, and fight our battles.'

Then Samuel agreed to find them a king, and the men went back to their cities.

Now at that time there lived a rich and powerful man called Kish. Among his flocks and herds was a drove of wild asses, and they were lost. Kish became anxious about them, for they did not return, and he called his son Saul to him to tell him to go and look for them.

Saul was a fine young man, head and shoulders taller than any other man in Israel. He looked almost a giant when he walked with other men.

Kish spoke to him. 'Take now one of the servants with you, and go to find the asses.'

So Saul and a servant went to look for the drove of wild asses. They hunted everywhere for them, but they could not be found.

At last Saul said to his servant: 'Come, and let us go back. If we do not return soon, my father will begin to worry lest we should be lost.'

The two of them were near Ramah, the town where Samuel lived. The servant told Saul about the wise old man.

'Behold now,' he said, 'there is in this city a man of God, and he is an honourable man. All that he says comes true. Let us go to him, for maybe he can tell us which is our best way to go.'

'I have no present for a man of God,' said Saul. 'We cannot go to him without taking a present.'

'I have a piece of silver,' said the servant. 'We will give that to the man of God, and he will tell us our way.'

'Well said,' said Saul. 'Come, let us go.'

So they went to the city, and asked where Samuel could be found. Soon they came to him, and when Samuel saw the goodly young man Saul, so strong and tall and handsome, he knew that he was a man whom the people would like for a king.

'You shall eat with me at the feast which is to be held in the high place outside the city walls,' said Samuel to the young man. 'As for the asses which were lost, do not trouble yourself any more over them, for they are found. You are the man for whom the whole of Israel is seeking, and on which their heart is set.'

'Why do you speak like this to me?' asked Saul, in the greatest amazement.

Samuel took Saul to the feast with him and made him sit in the chief place. The men there looked at the fine young man, and thought that he would be a good leader to free them from their enemies, the Philistines.

That night, on the cool, flat roof of his house, Saul and Samuel spoke together. Samuel told Saul how the people demanded a king, one who was strong and fearless. He spoke to Saul of God, and told him that a king must follow the word of God, if he were going to rule a kingdom well.

Then they slept until the morning, Samuel, the wise old man, and Saul the strong young man who had set out to look for his father's asses, and had found a kingdom instead.

The next day Samuel sent Saul home – but before he did so, he anointed him with oil, pouring it over the young man's head, and saying that God had chosen him to be ruler over his people.

And Saul listened and made up his mind to do the best he could. He went back to his home, and waited for the time to come when Samuel would show him to the people, and proclaim him as their king.

When the right time came, Samuel sent messengers up and down the land, telling the people they must come to him, for now he had found them a king. Then in their thousands the people came, and waited for Samuel to show them their first king.

And then Saul was brought before the people of Israel, and he stood head and shoulders above everyone else, a fine young man, with a farmer's cloak about him and a striped cloth bound round his head.

Then Samuel spoke to the listening people. 'Behold the man whom the Lord has chosen. There is none like him among all the people!'

'God save the king!' shouted the people.

Thus Saul became the first king of the Israelites. He left his plough and his wine-press, and led his people against their enemies.

20
David, the Shepherd Boy

Now, as the years went on, Saul ruled over the people of Israel, and used his strength and his might against their enemies. But after some while he disobeyed Samuel, and the old man was very angry with him.

Many times Samuel was disappointed in Saul, and at last he quarrelled bitterly with him, and went away to his own house at Ramah, not very far from where King Saul lived. Never did he go to see Saul again, but mourned deeply that he should have chosen a king who did not obey the word of God.

And then one day God spoke again to Samuel. 'Take oil with you, and go to Bethlehem, to the house of Jesse. For I have chosen a king from among his sons.'

So Samuel arose, and filled his horn with oil so that he might anoint the one whom God had chosen. He set out on the long ride to Bethlehem, and the watchmen of the town, seeing him coming, were alarmed.

'Now why should the judge of all Israel come to us?' they wondered. And they asked him, 'Do you come to us in peace?'

And Samuel answered yes. 'I am about to hold a feast, a holy sacrifice to God,' said Samuel. 'Call Jesse and say that he is to come and all his sons.'

Jesse was a rich farmer, with many flocks and herds. He was honoured that the wise old man should ask for him and his sons. He bade them all wash themselves and put on their best clothing.

Then they all went with Samuel to the high place outside the walls, where the feast was to be held. But before the feast began, Samuel told the sons of Jesse to come before him. And they came, fine looking men, fully-grown and strong. One of these was to be the next King of Israel – but which one was it who was chosen?

One by one Samuel looked at the sons of Jesse. But as he looked at them, God spoke to him in his heart. 'Not this one. Nor this one. Nor has God chosen this one.'

And when Samuel had looked at each of the men before him, he knew that God had chosen none of them. Jesse once more bade his sons to pass before Samuel, but the old man shook his head and said, 'The Lord has not chosen these. Are all your sons here?'

'All but one, and he is but a youth,' said Jesse. 'He is the youngest and he keeps the sheep. He is not old enough to come to the feast.'

'Send and fetch him,' said Samuel.

One of the brothers was sent to fetch the youngest brother of all. He was called David, and he was on the hillside, watching the sheep. He was only a boy, not very tall, with a sun-burnt, ruddy face, good to look at, and pleasant to be with, for he could sing and play music.

His brother called loudly to him when he saw him. 'Come quickly, David! You are to come to the feast.'

David was astonished and pleased, for he had been told he must watch the sheep. He sprang up and followed his brother as fast as he could, keeping up with him easily, for he was immensely strong, although he was not very tall.

He came before Samuel, his eyes bright with running, and his cheeks glowing red. Samuel looked on the youth and loved him. He knew at once that this shepherd-boy was the one that God had chosen to be king.

The old man arose and went to David. He poured the oil on his head, and anointed him. Now, when the right time came, David would be king of his people.

Then the feast was held and everyone rejoiced. David joined gladly in the feast, puzzled at what had happened, but willing to do anything that Samuel bade him.

Samuel went back to Ramah, and David stayed behind with his sheep. Everyone round about knew and loved the shepherd boy. He was fearless and strong, and he was a sweet singer, and could play his own tunes on a harp he had made for himself. His flocks knew his music, and would follow him as he led them from place to place, playing to them on his harp.

David looked after the sheep well. He was clever in using his sling, and could fling a stone for a long way, and make it hit its mark. Sometimes when a sheep wandered away, David did not go after it, but instead fitted a pebble into his sling. Then he would aim the stone to hit the ground by the sheep, so that, in alarm, it would trot back to the flock.

Once a lion and a bear came to kill his sheep. David sprang up and ran to face the lion. He seized hold of it by its beard, and then killed it. He turned to the bear, and killed that also. He was as brave as he was strong.

Sometimes David went to Ramah, and Samuel taught him many things he should know. He learnt to know the words of God, and he thought of them often when he went back to watch his sheep, and had all day long to think his own thoughts.

Now Saul the king was no longer a happy man. He was troubled because Samuel would no longer come to see him, and sometimes fits of madness came upon him, and frightened him. The only thing that could calm his troubled mind was music.

One day, when the king was gloomy and troubled, one of his servants spoke to him.

'Behold now, you are sad and troubled. You need music to soothe your unhappiness. Shall we not seek someone who plays sweetly upon the harp? When you hear the music, you will be well.'

'Fetch me someone who can play on the harp,' commanded Saul.

Then one of the servants answered quickly. 'I know someone who would bring you great pleasure. It is a young man, a son of Jesse the farmer. He is very good to look at, and is wise in many things. He is a mighty valiant man, and he can play the harp skilfully.'

Then Saul sent messengers to Jesse, and they said: 'Send your son David, the one who watches the sheep, to our master, King Saul.'

So David was sent for, and he prepared himself to go to King Saul. He took presents with him and went back with the messengers. They took him before the unhappy king.

Saul looked at the goodly youth, and loved him greatly. 'You shall be my armour-bearer,' he said. 'I

When Saul had one of his fits of unhappiness David took his harp and played to him

will send to your father, and ask him to let you stay here with me awhile, for I find it good to be with you.'

After that, when Saul had one of his fits of unhappiness, David took his harp and played to him. Then Saul forgot his evil thoughts and sadness, and smiled again and was glad.

21

David and the Giant Goliath

Once again there was war between the Israelites and the Philistines. King Saul ranged his armies on one hill, and the Philistines ranged theirs on the hill opposite. Between them was a valley in which ran a stream.

Now the Philistines had among them a giant of a man called Goliath. He was enormously tall and broad, and very strong. He was the most powerful man in the army of the Philistines. And every morning this man came forth from the camp of the Philistines and showed himself in his great might to the frightened Israelites.

He was a magnificent sight, for he wore a great, shining helmet of brass on his head, and a coat of mail upon his body. He carried an enormous spear, and before him went a man carrying his great shield.

For forty days he mocked at the Israelites and shouted to them. 'Choose a man from among your company and let him fight with me. If he kills me then the Philistines shall be your servants. But if I kill him, you shall be our servants and serve us. I defy the armies of Israel this day; give me a man that we may fight together.'

Every time the Israelites heard this giant shouting so defiantly, they were dismayed and greatly afraid. There was no man among them who dared to go against the giant Goliath.

Now David had left Saul, and had gone back to mind his father's sheep. When the Philistines marched against Saul, three of his brothers left his father to go and fight against the enemy, and one day Jesse wanted David to take food to them.

So the youth took bread and cheeses and left his father's farm to find his brothers. He knew where the armies were, and came to the hill where Saul had ranged his men.

He found his three brothers and was speaking to them, when the giant Goliath came out from the camp of the Philistines and shouted his scornful challenge.

David heard him in amazement. Then the boy turned to see which of Saul's men would go to fight the giant. But not one did. Many of them fled away and hid when they saw the giant coming.

'Will no man go to fight this Philistine?' said David in surprise. 'Who is this giant, who dares to defy us?'

Now Saul heard his words and was greatly astonished when David said he himself would fight the giant.

'You cannot do that,' said Saul. 'You are only a lad, and this man has been a soldier since his youth.'

'I have already killed a lion and a bear that came after my flock,' said David. 'The Lord God who delivered me from them will save me also from this Philistine.'

'Then go, and the Lord be with you,' said Saul.

Then King Saul armed David. He put a great helmet of brass upon his head, and a coat of mail upon his body. He gave him also a great sword to put at his side.

But David could not walk with so much heavy

armour. 'I cannot go with these,' he said to Saul. 'I am not used to them.' And he took the helmet off and the coat of mail, and laid the sword down.

He took up his own staff, that he used for his sheep. He went down to the brook, and chose five smooth stones from the water. He put them into the shepherd's bag he carried. He took his sling in his hand, and he went near to the Philistine giant.

The giant came on down the hillside, his shield-bearer before him. When he saw David waiting for him, he scorned him, for he seemed to the giant to be only a good-looking boy with a ruddy face.

'Do you think I am a dog, to be beaten with a stick?' shouted the giant, when he saw that David carried a staff with him. 'Come near to me, and I will give you to the birds of the air and the wild beasts to eat.'

Then David answered the giant boldly. 'You come to fight me with a sword, and with a spear and with a shield. But I come to you in the name of God, and he will deliver you into my hand.'

Then the shepherd-boy ran towards the giant, putting his hand into his little leather bag to take out one of the five smooth stones. Before he came within reach of Goliath's spear, he fitted the stone into his sling, and, with his sure and skilful aim, flung the stone with all his might at the giant.

The stone flew swiftly through the air and struck Goliath in the middle of his forehead, where no armour was. The stone sank right in, and he fell down upon his face. So David defeated the Philistine with a sling and a stone. He had no sword, but he ran quickly to the giant and took Goliath's great sword. He cut off the giant's head, and when the watching Philistines saw what had happened, they cried out in horror and dismay, and fled.

Then Saul's men ran down the hillside to chase them, and there was a great victory that day for the men of Israel.

David was taken to the king's tent once more, and Saul praised him for his great deed.

'You shall not return home any more to watch your father's sheep,' he said. 'You shall remain with me, and I will make you a captain of my armies.'

And so David did not go back to his father, but stayed with the army, the hero of everyone in Israel. He made a great friend, for Jonathan, Saul's son, loved him with all his heart. He gave the shepherd boy some of his own clothes, and the two went about together, dressed each as a prince, closer than brothers.

22
David, the King

David became a famous captain in the armies of King Saul. He went wherever Saul sent him, and behaved wisely and well. Saul was pleased with him, and soon set him over all his men.

There came a day when David returned from warring against the Philistines, with King Saul and the armies. They had been victorious, and the women of the city came out to meet them, singing and dancing.

King Saul listened to what they were singing, for he could hear his own name in the song.

'Saul has slain his thousands, and David his ten thousands,' sang the women.

Saul was very angry. 'Do you hear what the women sing?' he said to his men. 'They say that David has slain his ten thousands, but I have only slain my thousands. There is only one more thing left to David to possess – and that is my kingdom!'

And from that day Saul became jealous of his young captain, and watched him always to see that he kept himself in his place.

David's friend, Jonathan, son of the king, was grieved that his father should have turned his heart against David. Sometimes David had to flee away, when Saul had made up his mind to kill him, and then Jonathan would be sad, and miss his friend very much. When they met again they fell upon each other's necks and wept for joy.

Then peace was made between him and Saul and once again David played to the unhappy king, when his fits of sadness came upon him.

But one day as King Saul sat listening to the handsome young man sitting before him, playing and singing so skilfully, all his jealousy flared up in him. He put out his hand and took his javelin. He flung it at David with all his strength, hoping to kill him.

But David slipped aside and fled from the room. The spear struck the wall and quivered there. Then David knew certainly that the king hated him and would take his life if he could, and he would not return to him any more.

War with the Philistines went on for many a year. In one battle Saul and all his sons were killed, Jonathan among them.

Then the men of Israel went to David and spoke to him. 'We will anoint you to be our king,' they said. 'You shall rule over us.'

And so David, who had been chosen by God when he was a boy, was made king over Israel, and ruled over his people many years.

David took the Holy Tent of God to Jerusalem, and set it there. When Solomon his son became king, he built a very beautiful Temple, and his wisdom became as famous as his father's strength and bravery.

23
Elijah and the Poor Woman

One day King Ahab sat on the steps of his judgement seat, hearing what his people had to say and settling any quarrel between them.

As he sat there a strange figure suddenly appeared in the distance. It was a wild-looking man, whose long hair fell down to his shoulders. He wore a sheepskin cape and on his feet were strong sandals.

There were some there who had heard of this strange man. He was a wise man, a prophet of God, one who believed in the true God and knew his word. He had come to warn King Ahab that his wicked ways were to bring him punishment.

'As the Lord God lives, before whom I stand,' said the prophet Elijah, 'there shall not be dew nor rain for years until I say so!'

Then Elijah turned and fled away to hide himself, for he knew that King Ahab had given an order to kill all the prophets, the men who went about preaching the word of God.

King Ahab laughed at the words of Elijah. He believed in Baal, the god of the sun and the moon. He had had a wonderful temple made, in which he had set up ebony statues of Baal, and to these he prayed.

They were tall statues, dressed in purple and red, and ornamented with gold and silver. Ahab and his queen, Jezebel, bowed themselves down before these idols every day, and believed that all might and power came from them. They were queer gods to worship, for they had been made by man himself, and were only statues.

But all over the country men and women did the same thing as the king and queen, and bowed themselves down to images of Baal, forgetting the God who had so many times helped them in their troubles.

Ahab did not think for one moment that Elijah's words would come true, so he was amazed when the rain did not come, and neither did the dew fall in the evening. Each day the sun shone down, blazing hot, and everything began to dry up. Ponds, brooks and springs dried up, and at night and in the morning no dew was to be seen. It was a terrible time.

Ahab sent soldiers round the country to capture Elijah, but he was well hidden. At first he went to a rock gorge, where there was a small stream. He had nothing to eat with him, and no means of getting any, for no one lived near the lonely gorge.

But every morning and evening the ravens, big black birds who flew over the gorge, brought him bread and meat in their beaks. Elijah ate this, and drank from the little stream.

But when the little brook dried up, Elijah knew it was time to depart from there. So, pulling his sheepskin round his shoulders, the prophet climbed the hills of Galilee and went over the other side to a place that lay outside King Ahab's kingdom.

He came to a town and looked for the gate of the city. Nearby was a woman gathering sticks. Elijah called to her: 'Fetch me, I pray you, a little water that I may drink.'

The woman, who looked very poor, turned to go

Every morning and evening the ravens . . . brought him bread and meat in their beaks

and fetch the water for the wild-looking man. Elijah called again to her.

'And bring me also, I pray you, a morsel of bread in your hand.'

And the poor woman answered: 'I have nothing at all to eat, except a handful of meal in a barrel and a little oil in a jar. Behold, I am gathering a few sticks to make a fire to cook the meal for myself and my son, for we are starving!'

Elijah looked at her and saw that she was indeed half starved. 'Fear not,' he said. 'Go and cook the meal as you have said; but make me a little cake first and bring it to me, and then make some for yourself and your son.'

The woman turned to go, but Elijah still had something to say. 'Thus says the Lord God,' he said. 'Your barrel of meal and your jar of oil shall never be empty till the day that the rain comes again.'

The woman went to bake a cake – and to her amazement, however much meal she took from the barrel, there was always more left, and however much oil she used, there was still some in the jar.

Then she took Elijah into her house and looked after him, and there was plenty of food for them all.

But not long after that a great sorrow came to the poor widow woman. Her son fell ill and died. Now she had no husband and no son, and she cried out bitterly to Elijah: 'I did good to you, and took you in, and all you have brought me is misfortune!'

Elijah was full of sadness for her. 'Give me your son,' he said. The boy was lying on the woman's knee and she was sobbing over him.

Elijah took him gently from her and carried him up

into the loft, where he slept. He put the boy on his own bed, and then he prayed earnestly to God:

'Oh, Lord my God, I pray you let this child live again!'

And God heard Elijah's prayer and the boy stirred on the bed and breathed.

Then Elijah picked up the boy in his arms and went down from the loft. He set him on his mother's knee and said gently to her, 'See, your son is alive.'

The poor woman clasped the boy in her arms, hardly able to believe her eyes. But when she felt the child moving against her and touched his warm hands, she knew that he was indeed alive, and she cried out loudly for joy, clasping the boy tightly to her heart.

'Oh, now indeed do I know that you are a man of God!' she cried to Elijah, 'and the word of the Lord in your mouth is truth!'

24

Elijah Meets King Ahab

For three years there was no rain in the land, and there came a famine. King Ahab was troubled, for the harvests failed, and there was no grass for flocks and herds. It was a hard punishment for the wicked king and his people.

One day King Ahab set out to find pasture for his flocks and herds, for he feared they would all die. Elijah heard that the king was coming near to where he was then living, and he went to meet him. He was not afraid of him, and he thought that now perhaps Ahab would listen to his words.

So Ahab once more saw the wild-looking prophet coming towards him, and he shouted to him:

'Is it you who has brought all this trouble upon my people?'

'I have brought you no trouble,' answered Elijah. 'It is your wrongdoing that has brought trouble upon you and your people. You have forgotten the commandments of the Lord, and you have turned to worship the images of Baal.'

'What would you have me do?' asked Ahab.

'I will show you which is the true God,' said Elijah. 'Go now and bring to Mount Carmel all your wise men and priests, the eight hundred and fifty prophets who serve Baal and worship him.'

Ahab was afraid of Elijah, and he did exactly as the prophet told him. Soon the eight hundred and fifty prophets of Baal and thousands of the people of Israel were gathered together on Mount Carmel.

Elijah met them there. He shouted to the people: 'If the Lord be God, then follow him; but if Baal be god, then follow him!'

The people answered not a word. They saw the great company of Baal's prophets there, and they saw the king himself. On the Lord's side stood only this wild man and one or two more. How could they say which god was true? It seemed to them that surely Ahab's god must be the one to follow.

Elijah cried out to the people again: 'I am only one man, a prophet of the Lord, but over there are hundreds of Baal's prophets. Now hear my words, and do what I say.

'We will take two bullocks. I will choose one and they shall choose the other. These bullocks shall be gifts to the Lord God and to Baal, mine for the Lord and theirs for Baal. We will each build an altar, and on it we will put the dead bullocks, cut into pieces, but with no fire under to burn them.

'We will call upon our gods to take the gift of the bullocks to themselves by burning them up with fire from heaven. I will call upon the Lord, and they shall call upon Baal. And whichever God shall answer, then he is the true God.'

The people listened and answered: 'It is well spoken.'

Then the prophets of Baal chose a bullock and placed it in pieces upon the altar as a gift to their god Baal. Then they called upon Baal all the morning, crying, 'O Baal, hear us, O Baal, hear us!'

But there was no answer. No fire came to burn the

bullock, and when noon came Elijah mocked at the prophets of Baal.

'Shout more loudly! Baal is your god, and surely he must hear you! Maybe he is talking, or hunting, or on a journey. Or perhaps he is asleep and must be awakened!'

Then the prophets leapt upon the altar they had made, and cried out to Baal even more loudly, cutting themselves with knives so that Baal might see their blood and send an answer.

But there was no word from Baal, and no fire came from heaven to burn up the meat on the altar.

Then Elijah called to the people: 'Come near to me,' and they came. They watched all that he did.

There was an old altar there which had been built for the Lord God. Elijah mended it, and then he dug a trench around the altar. After that he placed the bullock meat on the altar and set wood to burn it.

Then, so that the people might know that he was not going to deceive them himself in any way, he bade them bring four barrels of water, and soak the meat and the wood and the altar in it. Even the trench was filled with water all round the altar.

He made the people empty the barrels of water three times over everything. They knew that no one but God could burn what was soaked with water, for how could a man burn what was wet?

And now everything was ready. Elijah the prophet went near to the altar and cried out with a loud voice:

'Lord God of Israel, let it be known this day that you are God, and that I am your servant. Hear me, O Lord, hear me, so that this people may know you are the true God, and turn their hearts back again to you.'

And then, very suddenly, even as all the people listened to the prophet and gazed on the altar, fire fell down from heaven and burnt up the meat, the wood, the stones of the altar, the dust around, and even licked up the water that ran in the trench.

Then the people were afraid and they fell down on their faces, for it was a fearsome sight. They shouted out loudly: 'The Lord, he is the God; the Lord, he is the God!'

Then Elijah went up to the top of Mount Carmel and waited there with his servant. He knelt there in silence.

Then he spoke to his servant. 'Get up now and look towards the sea.'

The servant went and looked. 'There is nothing,' he said.

'Go again, seven times,' said Elijah. And the servant went to look seven times. And at the seventh time he saw something. 'Behold,' he said, 'a little cloud is coming up over the sea, as big as a man's hand.'

'Go down to Ahab and bid him get into his chariot and go,' said Elijah. 'The rain is coming!'

Then enormous black clouds blew up and a wind howled around the Mount of Carmel. A great storm broke and there was rain everywhere, streaming down in slanting silvery lines. All the people were full of gladness, for this was the first rain they had seen for three years. The drought was over. The famine would soon be at an end.

Elijah sprang up joyfully when the rain fell. He ran down to where Ahab was now in his chariot. He girded up his cloak so that he might run quickly, and then sped, more swiftly than the horses of Ahab's chariot, down Mount Carmel, and right to the gates of the city.

25
The Man Who Left His Plough

One hot day in the autumn many men were at work in a big field. They were ploughing with yokes of oxen. The oxen worked in pairs, and the men with them shouted at them, and guided them round the field.

A well-known figure came to the side of the field to watch the oxen at work. 'It is Elijah, the prophet, the man of God,' said the men to one another, for everyone in the land knew him and his fearless preaching.

Elijah watched the oxen and the men pass by him at their work. He looked at the last ploughman, a man called Elisha. He was a good man, who had read much of God's word and who believed in God.

Elijah was looking for a man whom he could teach, so that when the time came for him to leave this world he might leave behind him one who would go on with his work of preaching to the people and warning them not to bow down before the images of Baal. For the people were like children, needing help and guidance in all that they did.

When Elijah saw the young man Elisha, and looked into his clear and thoughtful eyes, he knew that here was a man whom he could teach and trust. He walked up to him and put over his shoulders the sheepskin cloak he so often wore himself.

The putting-on of this cloak meant that he was

henceforth to follow Elijah and learn from him. The young ploughman at once left his oxen and ran after Elijah, who was going away.

'Let me, I pray you, kiss my father and my mother, and then I will follow you.'

Then Elisha said good-bye to his family and went to follow the prophet Elijah, learning many things from him so that when the time came he might carry on Elijah's work and possess the same wonderful powers that he had.

One day as they walked together, talking, a strange thing happened. A chariot of fire, dazzling bright, appeared between them, drawn by horses that also seemed to be of flaming fire. And, even as Elisha looked in amazement, there came a great whirlwind, and amid the fire and the wind Elijah, the great prophet, was carried up into heaven.

Elisha was astonished, and when he saw Elijah no more, and knew that God had taken him to himself, he was full of sorrow, and tore his clothes and wept.

Elijah's cloak had fallen from him as he was carried up by the whirlwind, and Elisha picked it up and took it with him, remembering how his master had placed it over his shoulders on the day he had been following the plough.

Then Elisha went on with Elijah's work, and soon was known about the countryside as a man who knew the word of God, and did many good works.

26
The Widow's Oil

One day there came to Elisha a poor woman, and she was crying bitterly. Her husband had been a good man, a prophet like Elisha, who knew the word of God, but now he was dead.

'My husband is dead,' said the woman, weeping. 'You know that he was a good man. But he was poor, and he owed money, and now the man to whom the money is owed has come to take away from me my two little sons, so that he may sell them as slaves!'

Elisha listened and was sorry for the woman. She loved her little boys, and no mother could bear to see her little ones dragged away from her and sold.

'Now, what shall I do for you?' wondered Elisha, and he thought deeply. 'Tell me, what have you in your house?'

'I have nothing at all,' said the poor woman, 'except only a pot of oil.'

Then Elisha gave her a very strange order, so strange that she looked at him in amazement.

'Go and borrow anything that will hold oil,' he said. 'Go to your neighbours and ask them to lend you empty jugs and pots, dishes and cups, as many as you can get. Take them into your house with you and shut the door. Then take your pot of oil and begin to fill the cups and jugs you have borrowed. Put aside all that are full.'

The woman left Elisha and did as he had said. She

One after another they were filled to the brim with oil

borrowed many dishes and jugs from her friends, and then she went into her house with her two little sons and shut the door. The boys brought the empty pots to her, and she tipped up her pot of oil and began to fill each jug or cup they held.

One after another they were filled to the brim with oil – but the pot from which the woman poured did not empty itself. Always it was full, and always it poured more oil as the boys brought one dish after another.

Then they brought no more, and their mother said, 'Bring me another cup.'

'They are all full,' said the boys, who had been watching in the greatest amazement, for never had they seen such a thing before.

Then the woman looked into her pot of oil and saw that it was now empty!

Then she opened the door and went to tell Elisha what had happened. And he said to her, 'Go, sell the oil, pay what you owe, and with the rest of the money live happily with your two children.'

So she sold the oil, and then took some of the money to pay the man who had said he would sell her children. There was still plenty left, and with it she bought food and lived in comfort with her little family.

27

The Boy With Sunstroke

As Elisha went from place to place, telling people of the word of God, he came to a place called Shunem, where a rich woman lived. She saw Elisha going by, and knew that he was a good man, a man of God.

So she called him in and gave him food to eat whenever he passed by. 'When you come this way there will always be bread for you in my house,' said the woman.

She spoke to her husband about Elisha. 'Behold!' she said, 'he is a holy man of God, and he comes by our house very often. Let us build a little room for him, and let us put there a bed and a table, and a stool and a candlestick. And it shall be his own place, that he may use whenever he comes by.'

Elisha was grateful for the little room. It was good, when he was tired, to be able to go to a house where he was always welcomed and where he had a little room set apart for him.

One day he spoke to the woman, and told her that he was grateful for all her kindness. 'I would do something for you in return,' he said. 'Is there anything you want?'

'I have no child,' said the woman. 'That is the thing I want most.'

'You shall soon have a little son in your arms,' said Elisha, and the woman was glad. Elisha's promise came true, and the next year the kind woman looked down with joy at the little son lying so peacefully in her arms.

She loved him greatly, for he was her only one. She welcomed the prophet even more gladly when he came, and showed him the child. Elisha watched the boy growing and looked for him each time he came to the house. The woman always kept the little room for Elisha, and the man of God was often there.

One day, when the child had grown a little older, he went out with his father in the harvest field. The reapers were at work and the boy wanted to see them.

But the sun was hot and the child should not have been so long in the terrible heat. Suddenly he felt ill, and his head ached so much that he could not bear it. He turned pale and went to find his father.

'My head! Oh, my head!' cried the little boy. His father knew then that he had sunstroke. He was carried home to his mother, and she took him lovingly on her knees, trying to comfort him.

But she could not make him better, for he was very ill, and about twelve o'clock he died. Then his mother took her little son and went to the room that she always kept ready for Elisha. She put the boy on the prophet's own bed, shut the door, and went out again.

She went to the field and called to her husband: 'Send me, I pray you, a servant to saddle me an ass, for I am going to the man of God.'

Then she left home on her ass and rode swiftly to Mount Carmel, where she knew Elisha was. She found him and sprang from her ass. She ran to Elisha and knelt down, taking him by the feet. Elisha's servant tried to push her away, but the man of God stopped him.

'Let her alone,' he said. 'She is in great trouble, and I must find out what it is.'

Then the woman told him what had happened, and Elisha grieved for her. He turned to his servant, Gehazi.

'Take my staff and go quickly on your way,' he said. 'Lay my staff upon the face of the child.'

Gehazi went swiftly. But the woman would not go with him. It was Elisha she knew, and Elisha she trusted. It was Elisha she had come to fetch, and she would not go unless he came with her.

So he followed her and they came to Shunem. As they came near the house Gehazi the servant came out to meet them. 'I laid your staff on the face of the child,' he said to his master, 'but he neither felt nor saw. He did not wake.'

Elisha went into his own little room, where the dead child lay, and he shut the door behind him, for he did not want anyone else there. He prayed to the Lord God, and then he went to lie by the child, putting his face close to him and taking the child's cold little hands in his. He felt the little body beginning to grow warm.

Elisha got off the bed and walked to and fro a little, praying. Then once more he laid himself by the child, holding him closely to him.

And suddenly the little boy sneezed seven times and opened his eyes. He was alive, and he looked round for his mother. Elisha called her.

She came trembling into the room, and the first thing she saw was her little child smiling at her from the prophet's narrow bed.

'Take up your child,' said Elisha.

The joyful woman flung herself down at Elisha's feet, hardly able to say a word. The she arose, went to the bed and picked up her little son.

She took him away in her arms, weeping for joy. She had not looked for any reward for her kindness to a man of God – but now she had been repaid a hundredfold.

28
Naaman and the Little Slave-girl

Naaman the Syrian was a brave soldier and the King of Syria honoured him, for Naaman had won many mighty battles for him. He made him one of his greatest captains, and Naaman was a happy man.

He lived with his lovely wife in a beautiful house. She was only sad when Naaman had to leave her to fight.

'This time we go to fight the men of Israel,' said Naaman one day as he kissed her good-bye. 'I will bring you back a little slave from the Israelites. They say that the children are beautiful. You shall have one to be your servant and wait upon you!'

So when Naaman came back he brought with him a little girl he had captured. She had the dark eyes, black hair and ruddy face of the Israelites, and Naaman's wife liked her very much.

'She shall be my own little slave,' she said to Naaman. 'Poor child – she misses her father and mother, and I will be kind to her.'

So Naaman and his wife were kind to the little girl, and she was happy with them. She waited on her mistress, bringing her water to wash her hands and holding the comb and the oil when she wanted to do her hair. She chattered about her home and her people, and Naaman's wife listened in amusement.

One day the little maid found her mistress crying bitterly. She went to her at once and asked her what

One day the little maid found her mistress crying bitterly

was the matter. Then she found that a terrible thing had happened. Naaman had been struck with a dreadful illness called leprosy, which nobody could cure.

'I shall never be happy again,' wept her mistress. 'Naaman is so mighty, so brave and so valiant – and now he has this terrible illness, which will bring him pain and death.'

The little girl tried to comfort her mistress. 'If only my master was in Samaria! There is a wonderful man there, who can do marvellous things. He could cure my lord of the leprosy, I am sure.'

The little girl had heard much about the prophet Elisha and all that he had done when she had lived in her own land. She had never forgotten it, and had often thought of the man of God, whose name had been on everyone's lips in Samaria.

Naaman's wife looked up. Could there possibly be someone who could cure the terrible illness of leprosy? She went to her husband and told him.

'Our little slave-girl says there is someone powerful enough to cure leprosy in Samaria,' she said. 'Oh, Naaman, if only it were true! Then we should know happiness again!'

Then Naaman went to the King of Syria and told him what the little maid had said. The king listened, and then bade Naaman go straightway to Samaria to the king, for he thought surely it must be the king that could cure the leprosy.

Naaman set off with a letter to the King of Samaria from the King of Syria. He went in his beautiful chariot, with his servants, carrying with him gold and silver and fine clothes as presents.

He came to the King of Israel, who was lord also of

Samaria, and gave him the letter. The king opened it and read it.

'Now when this letter is come to you,' he read, 'behold, with it comes Naaman my servant, for I would that you cure him of his leprosy.'

Then the king was afraid, for he knew that he could not cure such an illness. 'The King of Syria seeks to make a quarrel with me,' he cried in dismay. 'He knows I cannot cure leprosy – but when this man returns to him still with his illness on him, he will send an army against me!'

The news soon spread abroad that Naaman the Syrian had gone to ask the king to cure him of his leprosy, and it was told to Elisha the prophet.

And Elisha sent a message to the king and said: 'Why are you so troubled? Let Naaman come to me and he shall know there is a man of God in Israel.'

Then Naaman got into his chariot and drove to Elisha's little house, with all his servants. Everyone came running out to see the Syrians, and marvelled at them.

Naaman stood at the door, but Elisha did not come out to him. He sent his servant to Naaman with a message.

'Go and wash in the river Jordan seven times and you shall be healed of your leprosy.'

But Naaman was very angry at this. He went away, saying loudly: 'Does he not know I am Naaman, a chief man among the Syrians? Behold, I thought, he will surely come out to me and stand before me, and call out to his god, and strike his hand over the place where the leprosy is and make it better!

'Why should I wash in the river Jordan? Are there

not rivers in my own country better than all the waters in Israel? Why can I not wash in them and be clean?'

Then Naaman turned his chariot about and galloped away in a rage. His servants spoke gently to him, for they knew his tempers. 'Master, if the prophet had told you to do something great, would you not have done it? Then why should you be angered when he bids you do some simple thing such as wash and be clean?'

Naaman listened to them and knew they were right. He went to the River Jordan and dipped himself into the water seven times. And when he came out after the seventh time his leprosy was gone. All his skin was as fresh and clean as a child's.

Then Naaman was full of joy, and looked down at his body in delight. He went straight back to Elisha with all his servants, and stood before him.

'Behold!' he said joyfully, 'now I know that there is no God in all the earth but yours. Now, therefore, take a gift from me.'

But Elisha did not want silver or gold or riches of any sort. He saw before him a man whom God had healed, and who now praised his name and believed in him – and that was enough reward for the prophet.

So Elisha refused to take any presents. 'Go in peace,' he said, and went back into his house.

Then Naaman went back to his own land, and told his king all that had happened to him. When he returned into his house his wife ran to greet him, full of wonder and gladness to see him healed of his terrible illness.

And gladdest of all was the little slave-girl to think

that her man of God, and her own God, had cured the master she loved. How grateful Naaman must have been to the little girl who had brought health and gladness back to him again!

29
The Four Captive Boys

There was once a king called Nebuchadnezzar, who ruled over the great city of Babylon. He took his men and went riding to Jerusalem.

He besieged it and took it. Then his soldiers went into the beautiful temple that Solomon had built many years before, and stole from it all the lovely things that were there.

They not only took the silver and gold and other precious things, but they took also many people from the countryside and the city to be slaves in Babylon. Among these were many young boys, and they were marched off to Babylon, sad at heart to leave behind the land and the people they knew so well.

Four of the boys tried to keep together, for they were friends. They all belonged to high families, and they were fine-looking boys, handsome and clever. Their leader was Daniel and the others were called Mishael, Hananiah and Azariah.

The soldiers guarded the companies of slaves as they marched the many miles to Babylon. That great city was a wonderful sight to see. It had enormous brass gates, beautiful hanging gardens full of flowers, and a river that ran through the middle of the city.

The four boys marvelled to see such a wonderful place. They wondered what would happen to them there. Would they be set to work hard all day long?

Would they be beaten and starved? They did not know.

All the boys were put under one of the king's highest servants. He gave orders that the boys who came of high family should be set apart and taught all the learning and wisdom of his country, so that when they were grown they could tell their own people how great and wise were the people of Babylon.

The chief servant looked at the little captives in his care, and picked out those he thought were the finest looking and the best. Among them were Daniel and his three friends. Instead of being set to work hard in the city, or out in the fields, they were, much to their surprise, treated like young princes.

They wore beautiful clothes. They were given as much as they liked to eat. They lived in the king's own palace, and they had the wisest teachers in the land.

They were taught all the learning of that day, and they were clever and quick in understanding. They grew well, and their teachers were pleased with them. When the time came, the king sent for them to see what they were like, and if they were well taught.

The boys were brought in before him. He looked at the little company, whose faces were so different from those around. The little foreigners were handsome, with dark eyes and ruddy cheeks. Their eyes were keen and bright, and their minds were quick and clever.

The king was pleased with them. He chose out four to stand before him in his palace, so that each day he might talk with them. Those four were Daniel and his three friends. They were pleased to be together, and they answered the king wisely when he spoke to them.

Soon the king found that these four youths were cleverer than his own magicians and wise men, especially in the understanding of dreams. Like the Pharaohs of the years gone by, King Nebuchadnezzar believed that dreams had always a meaning, and he made his wise men tell him what his dreams meant.

But one day he had a dream which nobody could explain to him, and this was not to be wondered at, for the king had forgotten what the dream was, and could not tell it.

His wise men said, 'Tell us the dream and we will tell you the meaning.'

The king said, 'I have forgotten the dream. You are wise men, and you should be able to tell me not only the meaning of my dream, but also the dream itself.'

But it was impossible, and the wise men despaired, thinking that surely the king would punish them greatly.

It was Daniel who came to their rescue, and told the king his dream and the meaning of it. God showed Daniel the dream in a vision, so the youth knew it, and knew the meaning, too.

The king was amazed and rewarded Daniel with many presents. He made a great man of him, and allowed him to rule over the whole of Babylon.

Daniel did not forget his three friends, and he asked the king to remember them also. So Nebuchadnezzar gave them high positions too, and the four young men had great power in that country.

30
Three Brave Men

Now one day the king commanded that an enormous image or idol should be made. And it was made and set up outside Babylon.

'Gather together all my princes, governors, captains, judges, treasurers and counsellors,' commanded the king. 'Bring everyone before the great idol, and command them that when they hear the sound of music they shall fall down and worship the golden image that I, Nebuchadnezzar, the king, have set up.'

So all the people were brought before the idol, and waited for the sound of music to come.

'Whoever does not fall down and worship as I command shall be cast into a burning furnace!' said the king.

Then came the sound of music from all kinds of instruments, and everyone fell down straightaway and worshipped the image of gold.

But the three friends of Daniel would not fall down and worship the idol, because they knew that only God is to be worshipped, and they scorned to pray to an image of gold, that had been made by man.

This was told to the king, and he was full of anger. 'Call these three men!' he commanded. 'Bring them before me. I will speak with them.'

So the three brave men were brought before Nebuchadnezzar, and he questioned them.

'Is it true that you did not worship the golden image I set up?' he asked. 'Now when you hear the music, you must at once fall down and worship, or I will throw you into a burning fire. And what God can deliver you from a furnace?'

The three men answered at once. 'Whether or not our God delivers us from the fire is no matter, for we will never fall down and worship the golden image you have set up.'

Then in fury the king ordered the men to be tightly bound and cast into a fiery furnace, and it was done. Nebuchadnezzar expected them to be burnt up at once, but to his fear and amazement, as he gazed into the great fire, he saw people walking there in the midst of the flames.

'Did we not cast three men into the flames?' he asked suddenly. And his servants answered yes.

'Lo, I see four men, loose, walking in the midst of the fire, and they have no hurt. And the fourth is like an angel of God,' said the king, and he trembled.

He called loudly, and the three young men walked out of the fiery furnace. The king and his servants gazed at them in wonder and fear, for the flames had not burnt even a hair of their heads, and neither did they smell of smoke or of fire.

'Blessed be your God!' said the king. 'He sent down his angel to loose you and to keep you safe! Now do I make a decree – no one shall ever speak a word against the great God of these three men, for surely there is no other God who could deliver men in such a way.'

And the king made the three men even more powerful, so that they were among the richest and greatest in the land.

31
Daniel in the Lions' Den

In the years to come, King Darius, of the Land of the Medes, marched against Babylon, took the city and killed the king. Then Darius made himself king instead and ruled over the kingdom.

He set a hundred and twenty princes over the land, but over them all Darius set Daniel. Daniel had a wise understanding of the country and its people, and he had ruled much of it already. Darius saw that he was a man to be trusted, and he was glad to have Daniel by his side to give him counsel, and to help him to rule the country.

Darius showed such favour to Daniel and gave him so many presents, that the other princes became very jealous of him. They wondered how they could rob him of his high position, but this was difficult, for Daniel did no wrong thing, and was faithful in everything.

'There is only one way that this man does not do, which we may use against him,' said the princes at last. 'He will not worship our idols, but instead he prays every day to his own God. We see him open his window and look towards Jerusalem, where he was born, when he prays.'

'We will go the the king, and we will pray him to sign a decree saying that no man in his kingdom shall for thirty days pray to any god or man but to the king himself,' said the princes. 'We know that this decree will be disobeyed by Daniel, for according to his own law, he prays only to the Lord his God. He will not stop his daily prayers because of the decree, and then we shall tell the king that he has disobeyed his solemn decree, and must be put to death.'

So the princes went to King Darius, and asked him to sign the decree. 'I will sign it,' said the king. 'No man shall pray to anyone but me for thirty days. If any disobey, they shall be cast into the den of lions, where they will be torn to pieces and eaten.'

The decree was made known to everyone. Daniel heard it, but he did not obey it. Three times a day he opened his window towards Jerusalem, and three times a day he prayed to the Lord his God, as he always did.

Daniel knew that the decree had been signed so that the princes might get him into their power, but he did not care. He was not going to cease praying because the king had signed a foolish order.

The men saw him kneeling and praying and they rejoiced. Daniel had disobeyed the solemn decree. Now he must be punished. They went straightway to the king.

'Have you not said, O King, that any man who prays to anyone but you for thirty days, shall be cast into the den of lions?'

'It is true,' said Darius. 'I have made that law, and you know well that any law made by the Medes or the Persians cannot be altered.'

Then the princes answered in triumph. 'That Daniel, which was taken captive out of Jerusalem, and set up above us, does not heed your decree, O King, but we have seen him praying to his God three times a day.'

King Darius knew then that the princes had tricked him, because they wanted to kill Daniel. He was very angry with himself for signing such a foolish decree, and commanding such a terrible punishment if it were not obeyed.

All that day Darius tried to think of some way to save Daniel from the lions' den, but in vain. That evening the princes came to him, and reminded him that he could not alter any law that he had once made.

So, in great sorrow, Darius commanded Daniel to be brought, and to be cast into the den of lions. Daniel was brought, and the king looked at him sadly. There seemed no way to save this man in whom he put so much trust, and who was wise and loyal.

'May your God to whom you pray so much deliver you from the lions!' said the King, sorrowfully.

Then Daniel was thrown into the deep den where the savage lions lived, and a great stone was put over the mouth to the den.

'The stone must be sealed with your seal,' said the princes, 'and with ours too, so that none may save this man from the lions.'

Then Darius sealed the stone with his own signet, and the lords did too. Now none could save Daniel, for none would dare to break the seals.

Then the king went to his palace, sad at heart, reproaching himself bitterly for signing the decree that meant the death of Daniel. He would eat nothing, and he would not have any music played to soothe him. All that night he could not sleep.

When day dawned the king arose and went to the

Then there came Daniel's voice clearly from the den below

den of lions. He stood outside and sorrowed in a loud voice. 'Oh Daniel, Daniel, servant of God, is your God able to save you from the lions?'

Then there came Daniel's voice clearly from the den below:

'O King, live for ever! My God sent his angel, and he shut the mouths of the lions, so that not one of them hurt me.'

Darius could hardly believe that it was really Daniel speaking. He was exceedingly glad, and he sent for his servants.

'Take Daniel up from the den,' he commanded. So he was pulled up, and stood before the king, and to the wonder of everyone, there was not found any scratch or hurt upon him.

And then Darius wrote out a new decree, which he sent to all the peoples and nations.

'Peace be unto you! I make a decree. In every part of my kingdom shall men fear the God of Daniel. His kingdom shall not be destroyed, and his power shall be without end. He delivers and rescues those who love him, and he works signs and wonders in heaven and in the earth. He is the living God, and steadfast for ever.'